STANDSTILL PLANET

In their latest cosmic adventure, the Golden Amazon and her fellow Cosmic Crusaders fight to save the inhabitants of the planets of an alien solar system from destruction at the hands of the Zonians. Known as "the Accursed Ones," the Zonians are attempting a monstrous super-scientific crime—nothing less than stripping their neighbor worlds of air and water. The ultimate aim is to provide this stolen air and water for an artificially created super planet. Despite the Crusaders' best efforts, two worlds are destroyed and the Zonians seem unstoppable. Can Thania, an orphaned teenage girl and the new recruit to the Cosmic Crusaders, stop their depredations?

Another action-packed scientific adventure in the ongoing saga of the Golden Amazon!

THE GOLDEN AMAZON SAGA

STANDSTILL PLANET

THE GOLDEN AMAZON SAGA, BOOK 18

JOHN RUSSELL FEARN

Edited by Philip Harbottle

WILDSIDE PRESS

STANDSTILL PLANET

CONTENTS

THE GOLDEN AMAZON

by Philip Harbottle

In 1943 British writer John Russell Fearn decided to quit writing for the American pulp science fiction magazines, and to concentrate instead on books for the English market. Within a very few years he became established as a leading novelist in several genres, not only science fiction, but also mystery and detective fiction, and westerns.

His first new SF novel, *The Golden Amazon*, was published by World's Work in April 1944. In this story, a little girl of three years of age is made the subject of an idealistic scientist's illegal glandular experiments. The scientist's dream is to end world wars by creating a woman devoid of the usual lusts and frailties of mankind, who upon reaching maturity would institute a benign scientific rule. But the apparently successful experiment has a flaw: it instills into the girl a hatred for all men, and a ruthless cruelty. Her supernatural scientific gifts enable her to master atomic power, and practically leads her to destroy the world. She breaks the will and strength of men, and elevates women to positions of wealth and power. She also discovers human synthesis, and by this means she is able to escape retribution when she is eventually overthrown. She is seen to collapse and die, a victim of consuming ketabolism, echoing the memorable finale of Rider Haggard's *She*. In actuality, it was only her synthetic image, and this paved the way for the *Golden Amazon Returns*, and further sequels.

Fearn sold reprint rights in the first novel to the prestigious Canadian magazine, the Toronto *Star Weekly*. The magazine carried a special Comics Supplement, the centre section of which was a "complete novel," published in newspaper format. Aimed at a general readership, the novels were written by the top popular novelists of the day, including John Dickson Carr, Ellery Queen, and P. G. Wodehouse. They sold hundreds of thousands of copies, and the novels were syndicated to several American newspapers in the Maine and New York areas. The Amazon novels enjoyed extraordinary popularity (especially with Canadian housewives), and ran for the next sixteen years following the appearance of the first novel in the March 3, 1945 issue, ending with Fearn's sudden death in September 1960, aged only fifty-two. His final two Amazon novels appeared posthumously.

During Fearn's lifetime, only the first six novels were published in British hardcover editions from the World's Work in England, after appearing in the *Star Weekly*. This was because the publishers discontinued their entire fiction line in 1954. However, the Amazon novels continued to appear in the *Star Weekly*, eventually notching up twenty-four titles.

Fearn had resold paperback rights to the Canadian publisher Harlequin Books, but after publishing only the first three titles, they stopped publishing SF and other genre fiction to concentrate on their famous Romances line.

Meanwhile, as early as 1949, Fearn had realized that the Amazon series had the potential to run indefinitely. This presented him with a problem, however. The "origin story" of the Golden Amazon was conceived and actually set during the Second World War. Subsequent novels were written during the war and the immediate postwar period, and projected their stories only a few decades into the future.

He very astutely realized that to keep ahead of reality, he needed to move the Amazon *further* into the future—first into the outer solar system, and thence to the stars. So with the seventh novel, he introduced a new main character, Abna of Atlantis—someone equally intelligent, and even stronger than herself. These dynamics provided him with an *interstellar* canvas, thus ensuring that the series would remain ahead of reality.

Fearn's strategy was a great success, and the Amazon novels retained their popularity, ending only with his tragically early death in 1960. By then he had written a further twenty Amazon novels and made preliminary notes for his next (which would later be written by Fearn's biographer, Philip Harbottle).

Long after Fearn's death, his entire Amazon series would eventually see print from the pioneering US small press Gryphon Books in limited paperback editions, and later by the Canadian Battered Silicon Dispatch Box small press in their hardcover Omnibus series.

This new Borgo Press paperback series will be the first trade edition of all twenty-one of these later novels by Fearn, beginning with the seventh novel in the original series. First published in 1949 as *Conquest of the Amazon*, I have edited it slightly as *World Beneath Ice* (The Golden Amazon Saga, Book One) so that it can be read and enjoyed by new readers who may be totally unfamiliar with what had gone before. Subsequent novels have also been slightly edited for modern readers.

The publishers hope that this new series may create many more "fans of the Amazon." Meanwhile, any reader interested in seeking out the earlier six Golden Amazon novels will find that they are readily available on the internet, and in numerous earlier paperback and hardcover editions.

* * * *

To date, readers can enjoy the following new editions:

Book 1: *World Beneath Ice*
In destroying the threat of an alien invasion, the Golden Amazon had inadvertently caused a decline in the sun's heat, encasing Earth in an ice sheet that threatens to eliminate humanity. The Amazon encounters Abna, a descendant of Atlantis, stronger and even more scientifically advanced than she, and the ruler of an Atlantean colony still surviving in a protected environment on Jupiter. She refuses his offer of marriage, but agrees to form an alliance in order to restore the sun and save the Earth. One thing that Abna has not told the Amazon is that all the females of his race have been wiped out by a bacilli infection....

Book 2: *Lord of Atlantis*
A gigantic ridge of land rises from the Atlantic floor, causing massive tidal waves on either side of the ocean. Even stranger, both England and America are then assailed by an invasion of prehistoric monsters! A gigantic domed city rests on the newly risen plateau, whilst out in space an alien spacecraft orbits the Earth. Such are the mysteries and challenges facing the Golden Amazon, self-appointed

governess of Earth, as she struggles to unravel the maze of mystery that was the deadly legacy of Atlantis!

Book 3: *Triangle of Power*
The marriage of Violet Ray Brant—better known as The Golden Amazon—and Abna of Atlantis should have ushered in an era of peace and scientific prosperity to the people of Earth. But an unexpected turn of events finds Abna betrayed and marooned on a satellite of Jupiter, and the Amazon flung far beyond the Solar System. With Earth's two protectors removed, the planet is now at the mercy of another Atlantean, the master scientist Sefner Quorne....

Book 4: *The Amethyst City*
The metaphysical union of the Amazon and Abna results in the mental creation of a fully mature daughter—Viona. Quorne, still struggling for domination, forces Viona into a marriage ceremony, and impregnates her. But with the intervention of Tarnec Brodix, a super-mind from an external universe, Quorne and Viona are separately flung into an ultra-dimensional limbo. Abna chooses to follow after his daughter, leaving the Amazon to brood over the disaster, alone in the Amethyst City of Saturn.

Book 5: *Daughter of the Amazon*
A miscalculation by the super-mathematician Tarnec Brodix destroys his universe, and the fault spreads into the Earth universe in the form of a Dark Tide of Absolute Nothingness. Unable to save himself, Brodix transfers his knowledge into the one mind powerful enough to receive it: that if Sefian, the son who has been born to Viona and Quorne. Sefian rapidly evolves, and, no longer human, after saving the Earth universe, vanishes into the greater universe, to seek new challenges. Then the Amazon is confronted with a further puzzle—a large section of the planet Neptune is discovered to be an exact duplicate of the Earth!

Book 6: *Quorne Returns*
The bacterial intelligences of Neptune plan to conquer Earth by replacing humans in key positions with alien duplicates. The Neptunians are themselves subjugated by the sinister Atlantean scientist, Sefner Quorne. Alerted to the threat, the Golden Amazon hits

back by creating the ultimate doomsday weapon—only to precipitate a reprisal from the denizens of another universe....

Book 7: *The Central Intelligence*

The Golden Amazon's arch-enemy, Sefner Quorne, discovers that all mental gifts, such as memory and creativity, are something that is broadcast throughout the universe by a Central Intelligence—and then interpreted according to the quality of the individual brain of the recipient. At the surprising suggestion of his wife, Viona, the Amazon's daughter, Quorne travels with her to the very center of the universe, in order to wrest the secrets of mentality from the very source itself!

Book 8: *The Cosmic Crusaders*

The Golden Amazon renounces all ties with Earth when, together with her husband, Abna, and her daughter, Viona, she sets off on a journey to explore the cosmos. On the strange worlds of Alpha Centauri, she encounters Mizanu, the embodiment of evil—a planet-sized hypertrophied brain! Its baleful, crushing mental power threatens to reach out beyond the double-system of Alpha and Proxima Centauri to engulf the Earth and all the other inhabited planets of the galaxy—unless the Amazon can destroy it first!

Book 9: *Parasite Planet*

The Cosmic Crusaders discover a fantastic world of mental parasites drawing form and substance from our own Earth, fifty light years distant. The planet is ruled by a being identical to the Golden Amazon herself—but an Amazon who's coldly scientific and vicious, mirroring the original Amazon as she had once been early in her career. Inevitably, they become locked in a deadly duel—to the death!

Book 10: *World Out of Step*

The Cosmic Crusaders find themselves on a planet that seems mysteriously not to conform with natural law, a world out of step with the universe. It leaps ahead into time at unexpected moments, thereby suddenly adding many years of age to the flower-like inhabitants, and killing tens of thousands of individuals through death and old age. In trying to find the alien menace responsible, The Golden Amazon and her fellow Crusaders are flung backwards and forwards through time and space, threatening their own survival....

Book 11: *The Shadow People*

The Cosmic Crusaders discover a planet whose people are subject to a baleful influence from outer space that sweeps across their world—and for a brief while embraces every man, woman and child. It stirs the emotions of the sexes against each other. Men desire only to destroy women, and women men. Only those with higher types of mind are able to build a resistance against it. The struggle is dire and dreadful, and leaves its victims physical and mental wrecks. The less fortunate are left dead after the Wave has passed.

But when the Crusaders identify and destroy the source of the problem, they precipitate an even greater menace....

Book 12: *Kingpin Planet*

The Cosmic Crusaders are plunged into a strange new space, where all the probabilities of electronic law were strangely altered, a complete and stunning inversion of the so-called natural laws. They discover the mysterious silver planet of Tuca, and deep below its surface they find an enigmatic machine—the legacy of a vanished race. Masters of science, they had over-reached themselves by constructing a strange machine that could alter the very laws of nature and electronic probability. The machine had ultimately destroyed them, and blasted a neighboring planet into a cosmic cinder—and unless the Cosmic Crusaders can stop it, it may well destroy the entire universe!

Book 13: *World in Reverse*

Continuing their cosmic crusade amongst the stars, the Golden Amazon and her companions discover a planet in another space where living beings are being synthetically created. The mystery deepens with the discovery that the synthetic race is evolving backwards! Determined to solve these mysteries, the Crusaders find themselves up against the Mithons, a sadistic alien race led by a being known as the Supreme One. Can the Amazon save the day?

Book 14: *Dwellers in Darkness*

Voyaging into a sector of interstellar space plunged into total darkness, the Cosmic Crusaders encounter a powerful and sinister mastermind, who is regarded as a God by the race he has forced to evolve without eyes. And not content with shaping the evolution of their bodies, the mastermind has also impressed on their minds an urge to conquer and dominate…

Book 15: *World in Duplicate*

In the depths of the Milky Way, the Cosmic Crusaders discover yet another mysterious planet—this time a world that appears to be a duplicate of Earth, birthplace of the Golden Amazon! Their investigations uncover a sinister plot by an alien race that threaten the Amazon's home world with complete annihilation!

Book 16: *Lords of Creation*

At first, it appeared to be a sun, forming in space where none had existed before. It kindled as an atomic fire, sustaining itself by the breakdown of fusion energies. Then, even as the Cosmic Crusaders watched, the newly-created sun was no longer just a ball of fire: it was gyrating, like a stupendous Catherine Wheel, a flaming mss spewing filaments from its edges. Then they realized the amazing truth: they were witnessing the creation of planets, flaming streamers of incandescent matter that would condense into worlds! The Golden Amazon and her fellow Crusaders grapple with the very forces of creation in their most astounding adventure to date!

Book 17: *Duel with Colossus*

From outside the universe comes a terrifying threat. A colossal spaceship materializes in the void, crewed by master scientists who have only one aim: the total destruction of the Earthly universe which, to them, is but a molecule in their macrocosm. But the invaders have reckoned without the intervention of the Cosmic Crusaders—the Golden Amazon, Abna, Viona and Mexone—who pit their strength and scientific ingenuity against Lixom, the leader of the invaders—a duel with Colossus. But it seems to be a duel that the Crusaders must lose when, separated from their mighty spaceship, the Ultra, they are projected by Lixom thousands of years into the past, to materialize—completely unprotected—in the deadly vacuum of outer space!

CHAPTER 1

Petrified Planet

In silent perplexity the four figures in the huge control room of the spaceship Ultra stood looking down through the vast observation window upon a planet, one of five in a diamond-shaped system, lighted by a remote, golden-yellow sun.

To the four watchers, the self-styled Cosmic Crusaders, there was nothing peculiar about finding a planet, even in these far-flung reaches of the Milky Way Galaxy, but here was something definitely unusual—a world upon whose surface nothing moved. A world where the very clouds were motionless, where the strangely designed traffic was it a standstill in the broad streets, where distant smoke from tall chimneys hung like strips of dirty cotton wool against the sky. Motionless—inexplicable.

Then at length the Golden Amazon, leader of the Crusaders, stirred a little. She was a tall, unusually beautiful woman of apparently twenty-five, born of Earth and gifted by surgery with superhuman strength and fantastic scientific knowledge. She turned her violet eyes from the scene below and glanced towards her husband Abna. He was still looking at the strange planet, a seven-foot blond giant who seemed as though he aught to be a permanent resident of Olympus.

"Well, Abna, what about it?" the Amazon asked. "In two hours, or less, we'll be landing—if we want to."

"If we want to!" echoed the only other woman in the quartet—the copper-haired Viona, daughter of the Amazon and Abna. "There's no question about it, surely?"

The Amazon smiled faintly. "No, I suppose not. Exploration of odd worlds and the uplifting of civilizations in trouble are our business—so I suppose this planet comes into that category. But I'm not going to make the decision single-handed: we're all in this together."

Mexone, the tall, broad-shouldered husband of Viona, gave a shrug.

"If you want my opinion, Amazon, we just can't leave a planet like this unexamined. After all, we did see a fleet of spaceships near it, heading away into space."

"Yes…" The Amazon mused for a moment. "So we did."

She was casting back in her mind to the moment when they had come upon this world—the purest chance during their journeying through the Milky Way. The planet, through the telescope, had revealed its utter immobility, as far as surface conditions were concerned, and there had certainly been a fleet of spaceships of odd design, which had streaked away into space and vanished at an incredible speed, perhaps to one of the other four worlds which comprised this odd system.

Apparently the spaceships had not been *on* this particular planet: they had merely been traveling away from it, well beyond the atmospheric limits. But why? This was the thing that intrigued the Crusaders. And why were four worlds all normal according to telescopic observation, and the fifth one utterly paralyzed?

"Right!" the Amazon said finally, with a decisive nod of her blonde head. "We'll take a look, if only for the scientific interest of the thing."

She turned actively to the control board, and there remained, dividing her attention between the switches and the observation window. Under her guidance the vast spaceship cruised forward silently, the monstrous nose presently commencing to dip as the mystery world came into really close proximity… Then downward, with decreasing speed, towards the atmosphere in which hung the motionless clouds.

"There's one thing I've been noticing," Abna said, with a glance towards the Amazon. "Everything's petrified on this planet, and yet it is slowly revolving in the normal way. So is that remote sun—or at least it's changing its position, which shows natural movement. Whatever's wrong with this world seems to apply only to its surface…" His brows knitted. "It's the queerest thing I've ever seen. Utterly at variance with all natural law. Molecules must be in a condition of absolute suspension, yet in that case there would be zero conditions. And that doesn't seem to be the case…" He lost himself in bottomless speculations.

The Amazon did not offer any suggestions, nor for that matter did Mexone or Viona. Each one of them was wondering if anything abnormal would happen when presently they contacted the atmosphere. Would there be a violent explosion or something of that nature…? Needless fears. The passage of the mighty ship through the planet's air caused no disturbance whatever and, finally, by a series of deft maneuvers the Amazon brought the vessel down in one of the city's many enormous squares. Then there was silence as the atomic power plant was cut off.

The Amazon crossed to the window and joined the others in gazing outside. Like them, she felt the same puzzlement, and indeed also considerable wonder at the high degree of civilization the planet contained. Here, surrounding the Ultra, was a city that bespoke high achievement—a city of vast, skyscraping buildings, beacon towers, and flawlessly laid streets and open spaces. Above the streets again were pedestrian and traffic levels—and on top of the towering edifices, as the four had noticed during their descent from the upper air, were endless parks and gardens laid out with the precision that bespoke a high level of intelligence… Yet nowhere did anything move! It might have been a still, three-dimensional picture for all the animation there was.

Presently, Viona's keenly searching eyes settled on a vehicle in the street ahead. It was one of several which had evidently stopped dead in its tracks, but what made it significant was the figure half in and half out of the vehicle—a figure of a man, apparently, and entirely Earthlike in general physique.

"Whatever happened," Viona said finally, "it obviously came very suddenly—even before that man there had the chance to leap out of his vehicle. Or else leap into it."

The Amazon nodded silently, her eyes rising to skyline and the flat roofs against the blue sky. It seemed ridiculous to see smoke billowing up from somewhere beyond, ridiculous because it was not moving and looked as if it were painted on the heavens.

"We're not going to learn much by just standing here gazing out," Abna commented, crossing to the switchboard. "Let's see what sort of atmosphere there is."

He made a quick analysis and then turned. "We're in luck. Atmosphere's about the same as Earth, and so is gravity, humidity, and all the rest of it. We shan't need to take any particular precautions. Temperature's around seventy Fahrenheit… So let's go."

At his signal each one made an examination of their various weapons, then they loaded themselves up with provisions. Thus equipped, Abna pulled the switch that opened the airlock and then he led the way to the exterior. The Amazon came last, pulling over the external combination lock that closed the door immovably from the outside—a very necessary precaution.

"Might take a look at that man half in and half out of his conveyance," the Amazon suggested, and set the example by walking down the main street towards the phalanx of stalled traffic in the distance.

As the four advanced they looked about them, all the time searching in their minds for a reason for the freeze-up of everything, but as yet sensible solution presented itself. So they finally reached the man who was betwixt his vehicle and the ground, and in silence they studied him.

In height he was probably six feet: it was difficult to judge in his semi-crouched position. Between him and an Earthman there was no difference. Two legs, two arms, thick dark hair, an arrestingly wide forehead, and wide-open unblinking blue eyes that made him look as though he had stepped out of a waxworks… The Amazon peered at him intently then passed her hand experimentally before his face. He did not flinch in the slightest degree. He seemed to be in the grip of some advanced form of catalepsy. The Amazon desisted in her efforts and then felt his pulse and tested his respiration. Her eyebrows rose.

"Abna…" There was an odd note in her voice. "Abna, he isn't dead! His heart's beating very slowly, and there's a definite amount of breathing going on."

"And yet he isn't alive in the normal sense of the word…" With Viona and Mexone Abna moved to where the Amazon was standing. In the words of one Alice—'curiouser and curiouser'."

"It would seem," the Amazon said slowly. Prodding at the man's body through the queer neck to foot one-piece green uniform he was wearing, "that something or other has transfixed this man—and everybody else and thing—in mid-action. From the coldness of his skin I would say molecular stoppage is the cause, yet if that were absolute he'd be a block of ice…"

She sighed and shook her head. Clearly the matter was beyond her.

"Perhaps," Viona suggested, "there is slight movement really, so imperceptible we can't detect it. A sort of slow-motion world. I suppose it could happen…"

"Oh, it could," the Amazon agreed doubtfully, "but I don't think that's the answer here. Anyway, we can soon find out."

She took an instrument from her belt and attached it to the man's foot. Since he was in the act of leaping out of his vehicle his right foot was poised above the ground in a manner most fantastic. If he moved even a fraction the instrument would detect it… but ten minutes brought no change. He was immovable in the middle of a leap, balanced in a quite impossible position on one leg.

And this fantastic paralysis was evident amongst all the men and women whom the Crusaders encountered amidst the traffic. Some of the dead-stop positions were utterly incredible—as for instance the case of a young woman who, vomited from a stopped-dead vehicle, was in the midst of a mid-air somersault. And there she had stopped, an amazing folded figure six feet from the ground. Yet, when the Amazon seized hold of her she had no difficulty in setting the woman on her feet. But she remained like a dummy in whatever position the Amazon chose to place her.

"All of which seems to prove something," the Amazon said, as the others looked on. "Though life in the understood sense isn't there, there seems to be nothing to prevent us bending or shaping things to our own requirements… Certainly it isn't death, otherwise the bodies would be in a state of rigor mortis. Again, we experienced no difficulty in getting through the atmosphere, which shows there is no resistance in the molecular set-up. Yet clouds don't move and everything has come to a stop."

Silence. Abna, Viona, and Mexone glanced about them at the tall towers of the buildings limned against the motionless clouds. Each one of them sought for an answer in their minds—and failed. A planet of silence with everything truncated in mid-action.

"No suggestions, I'm afraid," Abna confided finally. "It would appear that these people are of a high order—their very civilization and the construction of this city proves it. And it would also appear that the spaceships we saw leaving the planet might have something to do with the present circumstances. Yet if it is some influence holding everything in thrall, why aren't we affected too?"

To this there was no answer. Then finally the Amazon began to move.

"We're not going to get very far standing here forming theories," she said. "We'd better have a look at the buildings—inside them I mean—and see if they tell us anything. Come on."

Promptly the others began to follow her, picking their way through the motionless traffic. In some cases the doors of the buildings were securely locked; in others there was nothing to prevent the quartet walking straight in, which they did—and the more they wandered through vast stores, offices, and machine rooms, the more they realized that these unknown people were very much on a par with Earthlings in the way they lived. Apartments were similar, and furniture was almost identical. Offices had a similar layout. The one thing different was, perhaps, in the machine rooms and factories.

There seemed, as exploration went on, to be in abnormal number of them for just a relatively small community. Every other building was a machine room, containing apparatus of prodigious size and unexplained use. All of it silent—all of it a glittering mass of complexity in the bright sunshine through the huge windows. All of it watched over by overalled men and women who had been stricken motionless at their posts.

It was about two hours later when the Crusaders came to a halt in the midst of machines. They looked about them in bewilderment, no nearer to answer than they had been at the outset.

"Only thing I can think of," the Amazon said finally, "is that these machines we see everywhere caused the paralysis—but how they did it we shan't know until we analyze them. At the moment they seem to embody principles that are quite outside our scope of engineering. For the moment I think we'd better borrow one of the apartments and use it as our headquarters. Then we'll start to work things out as best we can."

Decision made, they acted upon it and left the machine rooms. In a matter of ten minutes they were in one of the many opulent apartments, overlooking the choked main street into the city. Viona, usually in charge of the domestic department, went in search of what food there might be, whilst the Amazon, Abna, and Mexone stood gazing over the silent wilderness of paralyzed achievement.

"Whatever it is," Abna said at last, "we come back to one obvious pointer: the trouble is solely confined to this planet. The sun's moving normally and the planet itself is turning on a slow revolution. That seems to discount the theory that it's some kind of experiment with Time. It's something else—and as you said yourself the huge machine rooms we've seen seem as though they might be responsible."

The Amazon nodded her blonde head but she did not say anything. Then Mexone made an observation.

"There's one way we could find out. The Ultra is equipped with Time-traveling apparatus. Suppose we went back slowly in Time to the point where this world is alive again—then we could mingle with the civilization and find out for ourselves what really happened when the moment catches up."

The Amazon considered for a moment then shook her head.

"It's an idea, Mexone, but it's too dangerous. We might lay ourselves open to being caught in the same paralysis as these people, and then where would we be? In the same difficulty as they are. No—we dare not risk it." She turned her unfathomable eyes from the city and looked at the two beside her. "No, what we have to do is release these people from their trap, and maybe as outsiders we're the only people that can. I don't there ever was a more urgent job for the Crusaders—"

The Amazon broke off as Viona returned into the room. She was looking somewhat disgusted.

"No food or drink," she announced. "I found both, but the food is as hard as iron, and liquids just won't pour out of the bottles. There are taps, presumably for water, but I can't even budge them. If we want to eat we'd better go back to the Ultra."

"Food as hard as iron, and liquids that won't pour," the Amazon mused. "I wonder if..." A thought was obviously turning over in her mind, but, presently she shrugged it off. "Never mind, it was just an idea I had. I'd better think about it first... All right, let's get back to the Ultra and forget about making this place our headquarters."

In thoughtful silence they left the building and wandered down the main street towards the open space where they had left the Ultra. Each of them was busy with their own thoughts—then suddenly the Amazon stopped, and looked at her feet.

"That's funny!" she exclaimed, frowning, and the others paused and looked at her.

"What is?" Abna asked curiously.

For answer the Amazon retraced her steps for a yard or so, then came back to her original position. Finally she stopped and flicked her yellow-skinned hand back and forth along the road surface. Abna, Viona, and Mexone looked at her, then at each other.

"Oh, there's nothing wrong with me," she said dryly, "even if my antics do look like those of a lunatic. I've just noticed something— This street has a layer of dust all over it, yet we don't leave any imprints when we walk in it, and when I try to disturb it I just can't. It remains immovable. Considering that dust can usually be flicked away without the least effort that's a very singular discovery."

Her words set the others to work—and they found she was right. Even though the dust could be seen like a film on the metal and stone street, they could not shift it in the slightest—and also they made no impression on it as they walked on to the Ultra... And even at the Ultra itself there was another surprise. The vast weight of the multi-ton spaceship, and its none too gentle arrival had not disturbed the dust on the ground surrounding it—dust that lay on top of the soil and moss-like grass.

"It's beyond me," Abna confessed, as he followed the Amazon into the control room. "When dust can't even be disturbed it suggests tremendous scientific force at work somewhere. Do you think this planet is somehow enclosed in some sort of vibration which prevents movement—?"

"And we're untouched?" The Amazon shook her head. "No, Abna—guess again, Anyway, let's have some food and then do some more thinking."

Viona and Mexone promptly went to work to fetch the requirements of a meal whilst the Amazon and Abna stood thinking out the problem they had encountered. Trained scientists both of them they knew there was an explanation somewhere, but for the life of them they could not place their hands upon it.

"There's one thing we can be sure of," the Amazon said, when at length the meal was ready. "Whatever it is that's wrong with this world it's happened—but is not happening now. By that, I mean that the influence causing it isn't now at work, otherwise we wouldn't be eating a meal from food that is normal and liquids that pour in the normal way. The influence has made itself felt and is an established thing. It makes even the very dust motionless and liquids won't pour out of bottles. On the other hand, the people are only in a kind of suspended animation. They look dead, yet their bodies can be moved and their limbs put in any position. Whatever position they finish at is a permanent thing."

"Where does that get us?" Abna questioned. "We know it already, so how—"

"I was merely recounting to refresh my memory. We're agreed that Time itself isn't at a standstill, otherwise it would affect us as well and the planet wouldn't revolve." The Amazon paused and looked in front of her. "Science must have its basic laws, whether a planet be in the Earth-system or the Milky Way. That being so I think of only one possible answer to all this. It's a practical demonstration of thermodynamic equilibrium."

"It's...what?" Viona questioned, puzzled, and the Amazon gave her a sharp glance.

"You know what I mean, surely?"

"I think so, mother. Terrific mouthful of words, isn't it?"

"It's the technical term, mouthful or otherwise. Abna, I don't have to explain to *you*, surely? You know what thermodynamic equilibrium is, don't you?"

"Certainly I do. It means the condition to which all things material must aspire some day. It's the scientific name for a 'fortuitous concourse of atoms.'

"Exactly," the Amazon nodded. "All universes and worlds are less chancy today than they will be tomorrow. In other words, a world moves constantly into a state of ever-increasing disorganization, until finally all the shuffling of energy and radiation are complete and no further interchange is possible. When that state is reached Time as a factor ceases to apply and everything stops, unable to advance because every material change has been made. Entropy itself ceases to be."

Abna nodded slowly. "You're right, Vi, in the scientific particulars. Sometimes referred to as 'heat death.' The end of a world, of a universe...but you're not suggesting that such a state of affairs could occur naturally so quickly, are you? It takes millions upon millions of ages for that to happen, and the only places where it's likely to be present naturally is in certain dead stars somewhere in the universe. Certainly we've never encountered any."

"I'm suggesting," the Amazon said slowly, "that these people have, by some grave error of judgment, produced a state of thermo-dynamic equilibrium on this planet. It happened so suddenly that it caught them up in itself and made them incapable of movement or advancement. The very dust itself was affected—the grass, the clouds, and therefore the atmosphere. Nothing could advance any more because the limit of disorganization had been reached and no further interchange of energy were possible."

"But the effect isn't entirely complete," Viona said, musing, "otherwise the planet would be at a dead standstill and wouldn't even have a revolution. At least it still has that."

"About the only thing it *has* got," the Amazon said. "Otherwise every material thing is affected. How these people came to make such a dreadful mistake in their science we don't know, but it's up to us to release them. At present their plight is that of the living dead."

"You don't mean they're conscious of what's going on?" Mexone exclaimed in astonishment, and the Amazon nodded.

"I'm perfectly sure that they are. Consciousness would not be affected by thermodynamics. Yes, I'm sure they know what is happening but they're absolutely paralyzed and incapable of the slightest movement."

Abna stroked his chin slowly and then said, "I think something is wrong with your theory somewhere, Vi."

"You do?" She glanced her surprise. "Why?"

"Because our arrival hasn't altered things—and it should have done. It's an accepted premise that if you put a random element—even a pebble—into the midst of thermodynamic conditions, those conditions no longer apply because there's something new there, something that can be used for energy interchanges. More plainly, a something is there that was not there before, and the whole state of perfect equilibrium is destroyed. Surely you remember our experiences on Mexone's home planet, Voldas? Caused by your cosmic twin, Amazon II? So, our Ultra arriving ought to have released this world from the prison it seems to be in."

"Mmm, so it should... I must admit I'd forgotten our battle with that parasite planet..." The Amazon drummed her fingers on the table, dismissing unpleasant memories. Then: "That's a rather unlooked-for occurrence. As you say, a random element does destroy the thermodynamic state, so—"

She seemed about to say something further then she paused as the alarm buzzer on the Ultra's control board suddenly sounded. All four frowned for a moment, knowing that the radar-system only reacted when the scanner beam was intercepted—and on a motionless world there couldn't be anything to...

The Amazon jumped up and dived to the observation window. There was nothing changed outside—still the same vision of petrified traffic in the middle distance, and the massive grouping of edifices...

"There!" Abna exclaimed, at her side. "In the sky! Those same spaceships we saw near this world earlier on—"

The Amazon jerked her gaze upwards. It was plain now what had caused the radur reaction. At a vast height, possibly beyond the atmospheric range, there was poised a group of six spaceships hovering, undoubtedly investigating, but not moving.

"Who are they, I wonder?" It was Viona who asked the question as she came to the window with Mexone. "What do they want? And why don't they descend and make contact with us?"

The Amazon hovered over a reply, but for some unexplained reason she could not utter it. Something seemed to have hold of her tongue, her nerves, and even her mind, which made speech or even the formation of words impossible.

With an arm that felt as heavy as lead she put a hand to her forehead, trying to still the spinning dizziness that had come upon her. She lurched, grasped uselessly at the window frame, and then sprawled full length on the floor. A few seconds more, while she hung desperately onto consciousness, then that too deserted her and the rest was darkness...

* * * *

Nothing seemed changed when she awakened again, except perhaps the position of the sun, which seemed a good deal lower in the sky. Slowly as she realized that movement was hers once more, she struggled to her feet—and at the same time the fallen Abna, Viona and Mexone did the same thing. Baffled by their brief relapse the four looked out of the window. The only thing different was that the six spaceships had now disappeared and evening light was upon the city as the sun hurried towards its setting.

"What do you suppose happened to us, Vi?" Abna asked, as the Amazon stared with puzzled eyes into the sky.

"I've not the slightest idea. As far as I can tell we've had a blackout lasting about three hours. But how it was done or the reason for it escapes me."

"Whoever was aboard those spaceships caused it, that's obvious," Viona snapped. "Are we going to stop here and let them get away with it? It's pretty certain they belong to one of the other planets in this system so let's get after them and demand an explanation."

"And perhaps get ourselves into a mess," the Amazon shrugged "No—they can wait. We've things to do on this planet first, and the sooner the better."

She turned actively, but Viona caught at her arm. "Just a minute, mother. Don't you think you're taking the business of these space-ships a bit too lightly? After all, there was an attempt to do something to us, even though it didn't seem to materialize."

"For which very reason we can ignore it," the Amazon replied. "At least for the time being… Now come on, and let's see what we can do with the machines in the city."

She led the way outside and the others followed her. In a matter of minutes they had reached the nearest of one of the big factory-type buildings, and in the fading light they began a careful technical examination of the machinery, sometimes using one or other of the instruments they had brought with them. And all the time they worked they kept thinking of the six mysterious spaceships, so high above, which had mysteriously plunged them into a blackout—with what object?

As the daylight began to slowly die the investigation became more difficult. But at least the four had come to a definite conclusion. These machines were quite beyond their ken—which was saying a good deal considering their scientific know-how—and embodied principles that were foreign to them. Like everything else on the planet they were an enigma.

Finally the Amazon desisted from her efforts and looked about her in the growing darkness.

"To work out the intricacies of these machines, to say nothing of the hundreds of others scattered about the city, is an impossible task. With no knowledge of the mechanics involved we're up against a brick wall. I can only say that they're the queerest machines ever for producing thermodynamic equilibrium. The whole principle of them seems entirely wrong. They embody heat, disintegration, magnetism, and a complicated system that seems to incorporate radiation on a vast scale. None of those things is remotely connected with thermo-dynamics… They even seem—" the Amazon hesitated—"as though they might be intended as machines of defense somehow, though perhaps I'm wrong."

"I don't think you are," Abna said pensively, looking at her in the twilight. "These machines are definitely of a destructive basis, though what they are intended to destroy I don't know. I can make a guess—and only a guess. Maybe the travelers in those invading spaceships are up to no good and, earlier on, comprised a definite danger to this planet, so these huge machines were built as a protec-tion. But they were never used because the thermodynamic trouble settled on everything. The whole thing's an utter puzzle."

"Puzzle is right," the Amazon sighed. "Well, in any event it doesn't look as though we're going to accomplish much by just exam-ining these machines. We want to produce a revival somehow, and it looks as though there's only one way to do it."

Viona glanced. "And what's that?"

"I'll tell you in the Ultra. Let's be on our way: it's getting dark—and the last thing we can expect on this standstill world is illumina-tion, of the artificial type, anyhow."

CHAPTER 2

Captives

Back in the Ultra's brightly-lighted control room, the Amazon made herself clearer.

"We're agreed that the only way to restore normalcy to this world—if we accept the fact that it is really in a state of thermodynamic equilibrium—is to introduce a random element. And the only way to do that is to get a stone, or something material from one of the neighbor planets."

"Why?" asked Mexone, surprised.

"Simple. It is generally conceded—and proved—that all the planets from one particular sun contain the same materials since they all come from the same parent body, even as do human children from their human mother. Therefore, material from a neighbor world will be of the same type as this world, and able to produce the random element we want. We ourselves don't produce the random element because we are not of this planet, or even of this part of the galaxy, as we have already proved."

Mexone nodded. "I see, now. The Ultra acted as a random element on my world of Voldas because Earth is only fifty light years from Voldas, and formed from the same original nebula?"

"That's it," the Amazon confirmed. "We're in an entirely different part of the galaxy."

"So we fly to one of the other worlds," Viona said. "That suits me fine."

"Which means we'll probably fly into danger," Abna said. "That is, if we encounter the charming people who seemed to be in those spaceships... And all for nothing if we're wrong in our theory about thermodynamic equilibrium! If it's something else possessing this planet, getting a pebble from another world won't matter one jot."

The Amazon said: "You can take it as certain that thermodynamic equilibrium is the answer. There's proof of it. Those spaceships which attacked us didn't come beyond the limits of the atmosphere, did they? They took care not to mingle with anything of this world. Remember?"

"Well?" Abna asked, puzzled.

"Well, obviously, they knew that if they did so they might provide a random element and awaken things. They tried to be rid of us, by some process or other, but never for an instant did they make contact with this planet or enter its atmosphere… There will most certainly be danger, for even these unfortunate paralyzed people have erected vast engines of destruction to ward off any trouble—and have been beaten in the finish. As far as we are concerned danger won't be anything new, and the Ultra isn't exactly without weapons."

"Okay, then," Abna said, after a moment's thought. "Let's be going, then."

The Amazon moved to the switchboard and snapped the button that closed the airlock; then she switched on the atomic power plant. Without so much as a jolt the huge machine took off from the immovable dust, swept through the stagnant atmosphere, and within a matter of minutes was in the free void. In silence the Amazon surveyed the abysses ahead—the colossal, star-dusted backdrop of the Milky Way, and in the nearer distance the four other planets which comprised this unique system.

"Material from any of those planets will suffice," she said, glancing at Abna. "They're all from the same sun. But which do we choose with the least danger to ourselves?"

Abna reflected for a moment, then he crossed to the telescope. He peered intently through it as the Ultra cruised along slowly. Each planet, so far as he could tell, had civilizations upon its surface, pretty much on the same style as that on the paralyzed planet. Finally he looked up and spread his hands.

"Nothing to choose between them, Vi—they're every one populated. I'd suggest going to the nearest one and be ready for whatever may happen next. The nearest is about forty million miles away."

The Amazon nodded and turned to the controls. Immediately the Ultra put on speed, rapidly achieving some 40,000 miles an hour—which compared to the fantastic velocities it could sometimes reach—was considered a comfortable cruising speed. Even this pace was considered too slow for the Amazon for she increased the power even more, until finally the nearest of the four planets was growing in size even as it was watched, whilst the 'standstill' world was dropping away into infinity.

Viona, beside Mexone on the window seat, presently asked a question:

"Once we get to this world, mother, what are we proposing to do? Do we stop long enough to grab a stone or something, and then take off again?"

"That's what I'd thought of," the Amazon agreed. "A kind of hit and run visit before anybody can stop us—always providing we're not detected long before we reach the planet. I imagine that if we're pursued we've enough speed to give any followers a run for their money." She thought for a moment and then reached out and pulled a switch. Instantly it seemed as thought the Ultra was a mass of glass with transparent walls, floor and ceiling.

"Good idea," Abna commented. "Invisibility might help us."

It was not often the Amazon resorted to near-invisibility as far as the Ultra was concerned, but in past experiences it had proved an advantage. Power passing throughout the ship had the effect of reversing the position of the atoms on their axes, turning them endwise and thereby destroying the appearance of solidity. From the standpoint of a planet the Ultra was transparent, and having the background of space behind it was invisible.

For the quartet within the ship the effect was weird in the extreme. Beneath their feet and on every side of them there was no apparent barrier. They seemed to be walking, moving, and existing in sheer space, an effect that would have been intolerable to a normal person but which, in the case of the Crusaders, usage made commonplace.

Silent, surveying the planet that grew ever larger on their vision, the quartet waited. They observed this nearest world with growing interest, noting that in most of its details it was pretty similar to the paralyzed planet they had left. There were the same straight-streets, the same pedestrian and traffic-levels, the same park-like spaces. Only it was all alive and vital, with people and traffic on the move, aircraft in the skies, and clouds drifting in the atmosphere. A pleasant world, from the look of it, night still lingering upon it in a copper-colored crescent.

Finally, the planet was looming close. The Amazon turned to the switchboard and cut the power down to zero; then again she studied the looming world intently. Finally she looked at Abna.

"I don't quite like it," she said, and he looked up from surveying the vast; curving rim of the planet.

"Don't like what?"

"The lack of interception."

"That's easily explained," Viona said. "Obviously we can't be seen. That's the effect we want, isn't it?"

"Yes, but—" the Amazon made a bothered movement. "I trust to my instinct in these things, and I'm not happy. I know we're invisible, but a race that understands space travel—if this is where the space-ships came from—won't find invisibility any bar to instruments that can detect solids, such as radar. They'd locate us with that even if they couldn't see us—and they're not doing. It makes me uncomfortable."

Abna shrugged. "Okay, so we're perhaps sailing into a trap. We'll tackle that emergency if it comes... On the other hand this may be a planet that hasn't got space travel. If so, luck's with us."

The Amazon did not say anything; she had too much faith in her instinct for danger for that. Nor had she the calm detachment of Abna who usually looked danger right in the face and never batted an eyelash.

"Right," the Amazon said finally, and again gave her attention to the switchboard. "Down we go. I'll make for that stretch of open country beyond the city: less likely there'll be any interference there."

Still trying to shake off the feeling of worry that possessed her she brought the vessel swiftly down through the atmosphere, across the heart of the city, and way out beyond it to what seemed to be uncultivated land. The Ultra came to rest finally in a cloud of dust and the Amazon quickly snapped the switches that brought back visibility to the walls, floor, and ceiling.

"Well, all seems quiet enough," Abna said, studying the scene through the window. "Hills in the distance to the left and the beacon towers on the city edifices just in view on the right. As for the rest—nothing."

"Good." The Amazon switched off the power and then pressed the button to open the airlock. "Let's get some stuff quickly."

"There's no need for all of us to go outside, surely?" Viona asked, uncoiling herself from the window seat. "I can see a chunk of stone from here. I'll just nip out and get it."

She waited until the airlock had fully opened, then leapt lithely outside to the powdery soil. She glanced about her, noting subconsciously that the air was normal and the sunlight warm—then she dived across to the chunk of stone and whipped it up. With it in her hand she came back into the control room.

"A forty million mile journey for a piece stone seems crazy," she commented, depositing it on the table. "Still, there it is."

The Amazon examined it carefully, and then gave a nod and put it back on the table.

"Yes, that should be all right—of the same composition as the paralyzed planet, which is exactly what we need. Right, let's be off."

She turned to the airlock switch and closed it, then gazed in surprise. Normally, the lock should have closed ponderously and sealed itself—but for once nothing happened. There was not even the usual drone of power as the current was applied.

"What's wrong?" Abna asked sharply.

"Only that the power isn't working!" The Amazon's voice was grim as she worked the airlock switch up and down. "No, it's completely dead..."

She darted her eye over the banks of fuses but every one of them had a positive reading. Nothing wrong there. Finally, as the others grouped around her, she switched in the power plant—and there was not a sound from it. Suddenly and completely the atomic energy had ceased.

"Everything seems to be in order," Abna said, going over the various power outputs. "No breaks, shorts, or fuses broken..."

"But no power," the Amazon said, her voice edgy. "It begins to look as though my earlier premonition about trouble coming might be correct—"

"Trouble is right!" Mexone exclaimed, gazing through the window. "There's something coming. Look!"

The others moved and gazed with him, their eyes fixed on an object rather like a wingless airplane approaching from the direction of the city. It moved with the velocity of a bullet, finally descending swiftly not more than fifty yards from where the Ultra stood.

The Amazon turned towards the Ultra's armory, then she

suddenly relaxed again.

"No power—no weapons," she sighed. "We've nothing but the guns in our belts with which to protect ourselves," and with that she whipped out her proton gun in readiness as the others did likewise. Then they stood waiting, watching through the window as a group of four uniformed men came tramping across from the aircraft, glittering weapons in their hands.

"If they want to play games we're ready for them," the Amazon said. "In fact it mightn't be a bad idea to settle them without waiting to see what they do—"

"That wouldn't do us much good." Abna interrupted. "We can't do a thing with the Ultra immobilized like this, so we'd better see what they want."

The sound of tramping feet became noticeable in the control room, then without hesitation the four men entered, their guns ready. They paused as they saw the quartet waiting, their own weapons leveled. For a moment or two there was a grim silence, each party realizing that they faced an impasse.

"Well, what do you want?" Abna asked curtly, at length. "Or don't you understand our language?"

It was quite obvious that the men didn't. The Amazon glanced towards the Language Translator in the banks of instruments.

"Keep them covered," she instructed Abna. "I'll switch in the Language Translator to the battery circuit: that at least ought to give us an idea of what's going on."

With that she began moving. The men watched her narrowly but did not attempt anything. Still in silence they waited until she had switched over to the battery circuit and the Language Translator hummed with power.

Next, the Amazon picked up a device like a skullcap, bristling with wires leading back to the Language Translator. She placed the cap on her own head—to show that it was harmless—and then by pantomime invited the apparent leader of the aliens to do likewise. Instantly the amazing instrument scanned the language centers of his brain. The Amazon removed the cap and returned it to its position next to the Language Translator.

"Speak," she invited, and elaborated with signs. "Speak…"

She touched her mouth, caricaturing the formation of words, and pointed to the instrument. Finally, her meaning seemed to be apprehended for one of the men spoke in a curiously musical voice. To the ear his words were pleasing if unintelligible, but to the electronic brain controlling the Language Translator they had a meaning. As fast as they were received by the instrument's mathematical structure they were converted into English and spoken by an artificial voice through a loudspeaker.

"I am Imperix Iben Drass, commander of the President's guard, and I have orders to transport you immediately to the city."

"Does our language make sense to you?" the Amazon asked, and the Language Translator instantly converted her words back to the language of the visitors. They listened to it, and finally the man Iben Drass gave a nod.

"You are understandable. Now come with us."

"We have no intention of doing so, and you can't make us," the Amazon said. "Don't forget we're armed the same as you are. If you shoot at us, those of us not killed will settle the rest of you. Understand?"

"We only obey orders," came the stony reply. "It is not our personal concern whether you come or go free. I can only say that the President is unaccustomed to defiance."

"Then your President has a lot to learn," the Amazon retorted. "I assume he is responsible for the failure of power aboard this vessel of ours?"

"He has ordered a nullification of energy to be placed on your ship. It is radiating at this moment from the tall towers of the city, which you can just see from here. Our own machines use the planet's magnetic lines of force for power so are unaffected. In your case all electrical and atomic energy is dead and will remain so."

The Amazon did not speak for a moment or two. She silently studied the men, and the one who called himself the Imperix—or commander or captain, as it probably meant—in particular. The thing that surprised her was that they looked highly intelligent, smart, good-looking men, with no suggestion of the ruffian about them. Back home they would have graced with honors any royal guard.

"We do not propose to wait any longer," the Imperix said suddenly. "Come—"

He strode forward abruptly, his gun still leveled. The Amazon lashed out with her free hand and knocked the gun clean out of his fingers. He stopped his advance, his eyes on the muzzle of her weapon.

"That's just a warning," she said, nodding towards the fallen gun. "If I'd wanted, my friend, I could have killed you on the spot. However, I realize you are only obeying orders—but we don't intend to comply with them. In fact we—"

The Amazon was not quite sure what happened next. One moment she was coldly addressing the Imperix: the next he had seized her at lightning speed, torn the proton gun from her grip, and forced her into a kneeling position on the floor with both arms forced high up her back. The least sign of struggle on her part brought such unbearable anguish that she was forced to desist.

Even as she tried to break free—a matter that should have been simple with her enormous strength—she saw Mexone, Viona, and even Abna quickly overpowered by a few dexterous twists of the soldiers' arms and hands. They used either a form of Judo, or possessed far greater strength than they appeared...or something. Whatever it was, the Crusaders could not free themselves. More astounded than really hurt, they found themselves dragged to their feet, each one pinned with that excruciating grip.

"This is our only method since you will not comply with orders," Iben Drass said, and with a free hand he picked up the proton guns and tossed them on the table. "Now—switch off this language instrument of yours. You're not likely to need it again."

The Amazon found one of her arms released to enable her to switch off the instrument. In another moment she had done so, but a split second later she took what brief advantage she could. Bringing her free arm round she lashed her fist into Drass' face with all the power at her command. To her amazement he only blinked slightly at the force of the blow—a blow delivered with all the impact of the Amazon's superhuman muscles, a blow that normally would have smashed the bones themselves.

Abna, Viona, and Mexone stared too, utterly unable to credit that for once the Amazon's strength was insufficient. And by the time she had recovered from her astonishment the arm-lock was back and she was helplessly pinned.

Thereafter there was little the Crusaders could do. Forced to leave their guns and the Ultra exposed with an open airlock, they were impelled across the rough, pebbly ground towards the waiting aircraft. Without ceremony they were bundled into tae rear cabin, and only then were they released—but one of the guards maintained a constant surveillance over them with his gun at the ready.

Under the control of the Imperix the aircraft began to rise, turned, and then streaked swiftly through the air towards the city. The Amazon, crouched on a low wall seat, slowly straightened up and looked out of the window.

"Apparently," she said to Abna, as he sat beside her, "we've got more than we bargained for with this lot. Did you ever find men with such enormous resistance and strength?"

"Never," Abna answered quietly. "There may be something to account for it—not that it will do us much good. The unpleasant fact at the moment is that they have the whip hand. And the future doesn't look any too rosy, either."

The Amazon nodded worriedly, trying within her mind to think of a way out of the present predicament. But as she thought of every possibility there did not seem to be anything that suggested a chance of escape. In any case, with the Ultra immobilized there was no chance—even as Abna had pointed out. And once within the confines of the city the chances of liberty would correspondingly lessen.

Presently Viona changed her position and came and sat by her mother. The guard did nothing to prevent her, though he was continually watchful.

Viona said: "Do you think there's anything to be gained by making a dash for it when we reach the city? If we could once got free we night find some way of wrecking the nullifying influence which is holding the Ultra, and with that done we'd surely find some way to reach it again and escape."

The Amazon gave a wry smile. "Forget it, Viona. Trying to escape from men like this—and armed as they are—is an impossibility. The President, whoever he is, seems to have a very tough and capable entourage, I'm afraid."

"Then what are we going to do? Just sit down and take it?"

"We've never done that yet, and we're not going to start now," the Amazon replied grimly. "We'll act when we see a chance. Until that happens..." she shrugged her shoulders and gave herself up to looking through the window.

The guard looked at the quartet each in turn. Though he had not been able to understand what had been said, he was nevertheless suspicious. His grip on his gun tightened, but he relaxed again slowly as the four gave him no cause to be on the alert. They were resigned, for the moment, to accepting whatever came their way.

In a matter of perhaps ten minutes the 'plane was at an end of its short journey and swept down towards the sprawling city. The four studied the buildings, most of which seemed to be vast apartment houses. There were noticeably less signs of industry here than there had been on the paralyzed planet, but otherwise the layout was almost the same. Civilization, evidently, had reached about the same stage.

The journey did not continue down to one of the park-like spaces but finished at a rooftop where some fifty or so other planes were parked. The door clicked and the attendant guard jerked his head to the outdoors. One by one the Crusaders climbed out to the flat roof and stood waiting, surveying the sprawling majesty of the city from their high elevation.

"Looks like we're getting deeper in with every moment," Abna commented, close to the Amazon's side. "The moment there's a chance we'd better make a break for it, preferably towards those towers over there."

The Amazon looked in the direction he indicated. In the far distance, perched on three somewhat isolated buildings, which were probably powerhouses, were tall towers of skeleton metal, rearing to a height of perhaps two hundred feet. Plainly they were the same towers that had been visible from the Ultra and which, so the guard had said, were responsible for the death of energy aboard the Ultra. If, somehow they could be put out of action as Viona had suggested, then perhaps—

There was no further time for speculation. As the remaining three guards came out of the airplane the Crusaders found themselves seized and led towards a trapdoor in the roof. It opened by apparently automatic means and the four went down a long and curving spiral staircase, which gave a view into a dizzyingly deep well of doors and passages.

Everything seemed to be of metal. Walls, stairs, floors, and ceiling. It was only after a moment or two that the Amazon realized the place was a prison, a thought confirmed as, in passing, she noticed a balcony of steel-barred doors with complicated locks.

Final proof came when the guards opened one of the metal doors on the fourth balcony from the roof and pushed the Crusaders into the narrow room beyond. Almost before they had a chance to grasp what was happening they were watching the heavy door closing upon them and heard the click of the lock.

"And that," Viona said grimly, "would appear to be that! A nice, welcoming type of people, I must say."

She glanced towards the solitary bunk and sat down disgustedly on the end of it. After a moment Mexone joined her. The Amazon and Abna remained standing, surveying the metal walls, the solitary roof light, and finally the small barred window through which a pale sunlight was streaming.

"All the comforts of home," Abna commented bitterly, sitting on the further end of the bunk. "What's supposed to happen now, I wonder?"

"We'll probably find out before long." The Amazon reached up and tested the strength of the window bars. "Mmm, not much chance that way. They certainly make things solidly on this planet."

She was about to join Abna on the bunk when sounds at the door arrested her attention. Expectantly, she stood waiting, and in a moment the door opened to admit one of the guards and behind him an individual who, judging from the insignia on his uniform, was a person of considerable importance. Once again the Amazon remarked to herself upon his smartness and clean-cut handsome face.

Without saying anything immediately he made a motion to the guard. In response the guard wheeled in a barrel-like machine on a rubber-wheeled tripod. From the barrel depended a selection of cables, each one armed on the end with a sucker-disk.

The man of high rank then went through an elaborate but polite pantomime. He bowed slightly to the Amazon, pointed to his forehead, and lifted the cables up to it—then he tapped her head and raised his eyebrows in inquiry.

"He wants you to stick the cables on your skull," Abna said. "It's probably a language gadget—a less refined version of our own.... You'd better do it."

The Amazon nodded at the man's enquiry and put the sucker disks on her forehead at the positions he indicated; then when his lips began to move in speech there came into her mind, as clearly as though she was hearing everything with her own ears, the exact words he was saying.

"I am Rijilon, the—er—aide, as you would call it, to the President.

If you understand me reply in your own language: the instrument will take care of the rest."

Rijilon raised a spare suckered cable and applied it to his forehead. He nodded and smiled pleasantly as the Amazon answered.

"I understand you perfectly, Rijilon. Your apparatus is simply a variation of our own Language Translator, acting directly on the brain. Perhaps I can hold more sensible conversation with you than with your soldiers. I am the Golden Amazon of the planet Earth, and these others are Abna, my husband, Viona, our daughter; and her husband Mexone."

Rijilon inclined his head slightly as each introduction was made, then the pleasant smile faded from his face. He spoke again:

"I am informed, my friends, by the President's scientific advisers, that you recently made a landing on Zon, our neighbor world. Might I ask your purpose in doing so?"

"Purely curiosity," the Amazon responded, trying to make up her mind whether the man was as pleasant as he seemed or whether he was putting on an act. "It is hardly customary to discover a world completely paralyzed—so we investigated."

"So I believe. Did you find what you were seeking?"

"All we were seeking was an explanation, and that I believe we found. The answer has its roots in a scientific theory which on my world we know as thermodynamic equilibrium."

"Very interesting. But why should you be so curious?" A sudden hardness came into the voice. "Is it any of your business why a planet should be paralyzed?"

"It is. The four of us are the Cosmic Crusaders. We seek to undo wrong wherever we find it, uplift races that cannot fight for themselves, and overcome scientific barriers where they ensnare a people. A planet paralyzed naturally cries out for freedom, particularly as the people on that planet are not dead but are merely in a state of suspended animation."

Rijilon seemed to reflect for a moment. "Afterwards you came to this world. Again I ask—why?"

"We came to…" the Amazon hesitated, then she shook her head. "I don't see why I should explain everything, Rijilon. We came merely to—survey."

"I see. Most unconvincing, if I may say so. Having found a paralyzed world you left it and came here to survey, when your attention should have remained on Zon. You didn't come here to find a random element, perhaps? A piece of stone, with which to unlock the prison of thermodynamic equilibrium?"

The Amazon remained silent, her lips set. The pleasing smile came back to Rijilon's face.

"The guard told me about the stone you purloined from the waste land: he saw it on your control room table. When I reasoned it out I realized why you wanted it. I realized too why you endeavored to conceal your coming here—your invisibility in space, and so forth. The President adopted certain measures to be rid of you on Zon, but evidently they were unsuccessful. I wish I understood why."

"We are not so easily disposed of," the Amazon said quietly.

"Apparently not, but even so..." Rijilon shrugged, "Let it pass, it is of no matter now. The fact remains that you are evidently determined to be friendly with the immobilized people of Zon, even to the extent of reviving them, and that we cannot permit. It would seem, in the wisdom of the President, that the only way to stop your activities is to kill you. Regrettable, but that I am afraid is the price you must pay for being unusually clever scientists. We have already tried to dispose of you on Zon itself, and since that has failed we shall be more effective this time... I go now to report to the President and have his ruling as to what must be done with you."

The Amazon was on the verge of asking several more questions, but she did not have the chance. Rijilon detached the suckered cables from her head and his own, then with a polite bow he left the cell, taking the guard with him. The doer closed adamantly.

"What was all that about, Vi?" Abna asked presently—and the Amazon related in detail what had transpired. There was a grim look on Abna's face when she had finished.

"We've got to think of something, and quickly," Viona said, clenching her fists. "If they mean to kill us they'll do it sure enough. A crowd who'll paralyze a whole world will do anything."

"Yes, I suppose so," the Amazon agreed absently, and Viona looked at her in surprise.

"You don't seem very bothered, Mother."

"About the threat of death, you mean? Oh, I'm bothered enough, believe me, but it isn't anything new to be threatened with extinction... No, I was just thinking about something else. This ruthless sort of behavior doesn't seem to fit in somehow with a man of Rijilon's temperament. He is obviously a gentleman, and of high education. It all seems so peculiar—"

"Look. We're in danger of being wiped out any moment and you're in the midst of theorizing about Rijilon," Abna said, getting up. "We've got to act quickly."

The Amazon forced herself to be attentive. "I agree, but what do you suggest?"

"The window there, it's worth a try."

"It's too tough: I've tried it. Besides, it's too small to get through, particularly as far as you're concerned. You're not exactly a midget, Abna."

Abna gave a patient smile. "Vi, you're in the midst of a dream. You seem to have forgotten that we have tools in our belts even though our guns have gone."

The Amazon glanced down at the golden belt about her waist. For the moment she had overlooked the accoutrements she and the others invariably carried around. Abna for his part was not hesitating any longer. Standing on the bunk he whipped a small metal welder from his belt, powered by an atomic battery. He narrowed his eyes at the needle thin line of vicious blue flame as it bit into the window bars. In a matter of seconds, to his delight, the metal began to liquefy, and finally it boiled. In ten seconds flat he had one bar out—and with the Amazon springing to help him it took no more than five seconds longer to eliminate the remaining two bars.

A square space, extremely narrow, was left—with walls several feet thick. Abna's face became grim as he surveyed.

"We can't widen this gap: it would take hours with walls as thick as this, and I doubt if our batteries would last that long on full power either— You might manage it, Viona—and even you, Mexone. But that's all."

"At least we can try," Viona said, her eyes bright. "Even with only Mexone and I free we can do plenty. We'll find some way to get you out. I'm willing to try."

"Then do it," the Amazon said promptly. "Outside you get."

Viona leapt lightly onto the bunk, then with Abna's hands supporting her shoulders she thrust her legs through the small opening. Gently she was eased through, with very little room to spare, her arms extended over her head to reduce her width to the minimum. And at length she had slipped through the gap and vanished. Where to, those in the cell did not know: they could only pray that she had not plunged to her death.

Anything but it, as a matter of fact. She had dropped some twelve feet to a flat roof overlooking the city and it being too far down for her to get back to the cell window she could only watch as Mexone's feet and legs came wriggling into view. Being bulkier than Viona he had something of a desperate struggle, particularly with his shoulders—but finally he managed it despite gashes and cuts. He came sliding through and dropped the twelve feet to the rooftop at Viona's side.

"Okay?" she asked, helping him up.

"Yes—I'm all right." He rubbed his bruises and looked at the skin grazes and cuts visible through his torn shirt. "What's the next move?"

"Get mother and father out as fast as we can…" Viona looked quickly about her. "Our escape doesn't seem to have been noticed, anyway…"

She hurried to the edge of the roof and looked over the parapet onto the sprawling city. It went down for a thousand feet in great canyons of metal and stone.

"Nothing we can do that way," she said, as Mexone came to her side. "I was thinking how we might get into the building again, then make for the door of the cell where mother and father are. We could probably blast the lock with our welders—"

"To get in the building there's only one way—climb up to the roof and go down through the trapdoor where we were taken at first. And let's hope we're not seen."

Viona turned her back on the street and appraised the lofty bulk of the prison building. It went up for about three hundred feet, its smooth face marked out with the windows of cells. The only possible way up to the flat roof was by means of a thick power cable. Viona followed it with her eyes. It was attached to an aircraft beacon on the roof, and then down in a slack curve over the city itself, and its nearest proximity was at least fifty feet.

"Any suggestions?" she asked. "Beyond turning ourselves into kangaroos?"

"Only one way," Mexone said grimly. "We can't jump up to this cable, but we might be able to jump down to it. Let's see where it goes."

He hurried to the parapet and stared below. Viona joined him, then they exchanged anxious looks. The cable, after depending fifty feet above the roof on which they stood, went across the canyon of street, and after that away towards the city itself. From the parapet to the cable was a distance of perhaps thirty feet.

"You mean…" Viona hesitated. "Jump down to it? Catch hold of it?"

"There's no other way to get up to that roof. I know the risk. If we miss in our jump it's a thousand feet down to death. If we catch on we stand a chance of going hand over hand up to the roof."

"And if there's power in the cable, as there probably will be?"

"We shan't come to harm unless we touch anything and complete the circuit. You should know that. Swinging free we'll be all right, the same as birds are all right when they perch on a high tension wire."

There was silence for a moment as they each weighed up the situation—risky in every sense of the word. Then at last Viona gave a shrug and braced herself.

"It's got to be done, Mexone. We can't stop here and mother and dad are waiting for us to do something. If by any chance we're seen swinging on the wire we'll make beautiful targets, but that's a risk we'll have to take."

She climbed up on to the parapet and tightened the belt about her slacks. For a moment or two she stood judging the distance and tried not to look at the yawning canyon between the buildings. Then she leapt—her hands outflung.

The sensation was terrifying. She seemed to go down forever, and for ghastly seconds imagined she'd misjudged her objective—then she hit it with one hand and swung dizzily in space as the wire jolted under the impact. Instantly she brought round her other hand and hung on desperately, aware of this awful slack hoop reaching up into the very skies.

She waited a moment or two until the swinging of the wire became steadier—then she began to move slowly upwards, hand over hand, calling on every ounce of her superb strength to sustain her in the effort. She needed it, every scrap. Any normal girl would never been able to make the sustained effort, but back of Viona was the same iron strength as her mother, to say nothing of the same determination.

She did not glance below at Mexone: in fact she did not look anywhere except the building towards which she was struggling and the blue sky and the wire above her clenched hands…

Then suddenly Mexone must have leapt and reached the wire. It bounced so violently as his weight hit it that Viona nearly lost her grip. For a moment she hung, the dizzying depths below her, and with her eyes shut in horror—then ever so slowly the jolting of the wire began to calm down and she went on again.

CHAPTER 3

Escape

Slowly, gradually, until even her accustomed muscles ached, Viona went on. She went in fear, too, of being detected at any moment—but nothing happened. Nor was there a chance to rest, for this only meant letting her weight pull on her tortured arms—so hand over hand she went, Mexone at a not very great distance behind, until at last she realized she was over the flat roof where the airplanes were parked. She glanced about her, then let herself drop. She fell heavily, breathing hard, and stood for a moment half crouched and regaining her strength.

Moments later Mexone dropped too. He gave a relieved grin and hugged her to him for a moment.

"Done it! Everything else should be child's play compared to that."

Viona rubbed her aching shoulders and looked about her upon the parked airplanes. After a moment she spoke her thoughts.

"I wonder if Rijilon is still in the building somewhere, or whether he'll arrive in an airplane and go down through the trapdoor to the cells? Our future actions depend on what he's going to do."

"He said something about going to report to the President, didn't he, so he could decide what is to be done with us? Or so your mother said, translating his language."

"So he did!" Viona's eyes brightened. "Well, the President is hardly likely to be in a huge prison building like this is. We'll wait for him: he'll probably turn up before long."

"And when he does? Don't forget the strength of these people and the fact that we've got no guns."

"We'll use our metal welders in place of guns: I don't think anybody will want to argue with those. If we can only take him by surprise we can—and will—do a good deal. Once get mother and father free and they'll know how to handle the situation…"

Mexone nodded, not very hopefully—then he jerked his head in the direction of a nearby group of parked machines.

"Better get behind those for concealment—" He broke off and stared at the sky over the distant city. "Look! There's a plane coming this way— Quick! Out of sight!"

Immediately they hurried, keeping low to the roof, and from the shelter of the parked planes they watched the distant aircraft come nearer, circle once, and then drop helicopter-wise to the flat space below. The hum of the engines stopped and two pairs of keen eyes watched Rijilon himself, lordly and majestic, alight from the 'plane and move with dignified tread towards the distant trapdoor. A guard—the same one who had accompanied him before—came into view a moment later, carrying the now folded language machine in one hand.

Viona waited until both men had disappeared through the trap-door then she gave Mexone a glance.

"Come on—and make as little noise as possible."

When presently they gained the trapdoor opening and peered through it they beheld Rijilon and the guard half way down the first section of spiral staircase. Viona did not hesitate a moment. She jumped forward to the rail of the stairs, poised herself upon it, and then dropped with thunderbolt swiftness. The guard did not stand a chance—he never expected the hurtling woman who landed on top of him, her feet jolting him in the small of his back, setting the Language machine tumbling out of his hands and clattering into the deep well below, he went reeling head over heels down the staircase.

Rijilon did not do anything for the moment: he was too astounded. It was only when a sledgehammer blow from Viona sent the demoral-ized guard toppling over the rail into the depths below that he came to life. He whipped out a gun, but in that time Mexone had reached him from behind and was jabbing the welder between his shoulder blades.

Viona turned, thankful that she had disposed of the guard before he had had a chance to use his Judo-grip and incredible strength. She faced Rijilon and made a motion to him. His gun dropped from his fingers to the metal stairs. Viona smiled and picked it up, leveling it, her finger just touching the unfamiliar button.

Rijilon straightened—obviously somewhat scared but still the master of his dignity. Viona came up to him, a cold smile on her face. With her own welder she indicated that he was to move.

"Get moving to my mother—the Golden Amazon," Viona ordered.

Rijilon hesitated, the words 'Golden Amazon' registering in his mind. Then with a little, helpless gesture he complied with Viona's wishes and marched down the stairs, pausing only once to look into the well at the dim sprawled figure of the guard far below.

Whether he was dead or not, Viona did not know—nor did she care. The release of her parents was the main thing on her mind.

So, finally, the cell of the Amazon and Abna was reached. Rijilon, grim faced, opened the complicated lock and the door swung inwards. Slowly, ready for any trouble the Amazon and Abna came into view—then they relaxed and smiled as they saw Viona and Mexone with their welders leveled.

"Explanations can come later, mother," Viona said briefly. "We've got to get clear of this building as quickly as we can—"

She gave Rijilon a shove and sent him stumbling into the cell; then she slammed and locked the door upon him.

"Now what?" the Amazon asked, glancing quickly about her.

"Up to the roof. We can grab one of those planes and do our best to wreck the towers issuing that nullifying energy—then to the Ultra as quick as we can. Let's go."

Viona swung and raced away up the passage, the Amazon close beside her. As they hurried up the spiral staircase the Amazon hurried through a series of questions.

"You're not hurt, are you, Viona?"

"I'm fine."

"Good! How did you manage to get into the building again?"

"Mexone and I swung on a high tension wire, and it was no picnic. The rest was luck—Rijilon coming when he did, along with a guard."

"Guard! Where is he now?"

Viona grinned, "Down in the stair well somewhere. I knocked him over the rail."

There was no chance for further conversation: they had come to the top of the staircase, and of course the trapdoor opening. In another moment they were out on the flat roof.

"This prison building seems to be very quiet," Abna said, musing. "Wonder why it is? If there's anybody in the other cells they certainly don't make much noise—and I've seen no sign of a guard anywhere."

"A prison building that has no inmates seems to speak well for the good behavior of the citizens," the Amazon replied. "Anyway, that's as it may be—We've got ourselves to consider before we're spotted."

"We'll take that 'plane," Viona, said, nodding to the aircraft in which Rijilon and the guard had arrived. "The cabin door's still open."

She sped across the roof and climbed into the plane's interior, her mother, Abna, and Mexone close behind. Once the doer was shut the Amazon settled in the driving seat and studied the controls.

"We can discover how to fly it, surely?" Viona asked, looking over her mother's shoulder. "Didn't Imperix Ibben Drass say that they used magnetic lines of force for propulsion so the tower's nullifying energy wouldn't affect them?"

"Yes; but I assumed he was referring to spaceships."

"And aircraft as well, I think," Viona said. "There's no sign of an atomic power plant, and I'm pretty sure they don't use old-fashioned gasoline or jets aboard this craft."

The Amazon studied the controls for a while longer, then at last she grasped a significant-looking red lever and pulled on it gently. Instantly a power plant came to life somewhere in the structure of the ship.

"Right so far," the Amazon murmured. "Now to risk a takeoff."

She reasoned out which she believed was the correct lever and pulled it. Instantly the craft lifted lightly and shot diagonally towards the roof parapet. The Amazon pulled the control further back and the hurtling machine missed the stone and metalwork by a matter of a few feet. Then they were hurtling across the mass of the city at dizzying speed, until the Amazon found how to cut down the acceleration.

"Good!" the Amazon murmured. "Everything's under control at the moment. I've got the hang of it now—" She looked ahead through the observation window. "We want to destroy the nullifying effect, but how do we know which tower it is?"

"Circle each one," Abna said, pulling an instrument from his belt. "I'll be able to discover with this detector which one is issuing a radiation. Then we'll think further."

The Amazon obeyed, the aircraft now completely under her control. Both she and the others watched anxiously as, now and again, they beheld other aircraft cleaving through the sky—but they did not make any attempt to molest, or even investigate. After all, they had no reason to, and at the moment Rijilon was imprisoned in a cell from which he could not possibly escape—even through the window. He was too well proportioned for that.

But liberty could not last forever, the quartet realized—so they had to complete the task on hand quickly as possible.

Before long the first of the three towers came close. The Amazon moved the switches and the aircraft swung round in a steep bank circumnavigating the first of the towers in a matter of moments. Abna stood with his detector in his hand, watching for interference, but none made itself evident.

"Try the middle one," he said, as the Amazon glanced at him inquiringly.

She did—and this gave forth no results. But on the final one there was a distinct reaction. Abna gave a murmur of delight.

"This is the one." He put his instrument away. "Think you can lower this machine to within a few feet of the tower top?"

"It should be possible," Viona said. "When Rijilon arrived this machine came down to the roof like a helicopter."

"I'll do my best," the Amazon said, studying the switch layout. "If I can do it what do you propose doing?"

"Wrecking the source of the energy," Abna answered promptly. "Everything depends on speed on this occasion—so I'll find the main cable, cut it with my welder, and be back in the plane directly. After that—the Ultra as fast as we can go."

The Amazon nodded and juggled the switches. The 'plane went through the most amazing gyrations and aerobatics until she found the right controls: once this was mastered she swept downwards and forwards with ever decreasing speed until the tower top loomed dead in front. Velocity dropped to zero and she began to lower the craft, foot by foot, whilst Abna wrenched open the cabin door and stood ready to jump, his welder in his hand.

"Here, dad, take this." Viona thrust Rijilon's gun into his hand. "Never know what you might need."

Abna flashed a brief glance of thanks, and then jumped. He landed heavily on metal grating, struggled up, and looked around him. At the moment there was nobody in sight, and overhead, still lowering gently, was the bulk of the airplane, Viona and Mexone watching intently in the open cabin doorway.

To Abna, the top of the tower—perched two hundred feet above the building on which it stood, a building that was probably a power-house—suggested a lighthouse. There was a similar vast lamp organization in the skeleton metalwork, and a similar maze of lenses with faceted fronts. Whatever energy was being emanated was not visible to the eye, but it was there. The detectors had said so, and since it was influencing the Ultra—which Abna could see vaguely as a gray speck in the deserted countryside in the distance—it was probably on the side of the lens contraption turned away from him.

This he did not trouble to ascertain. His interest was taken almost immediately by two thick cables leading from the lamp device into the depths of the tower—going down and down amidst the skeletal metalwork until they vanished through the roof of the building proper.

Abna grinned, pressed the button on his welder, and sent the needle-thin flame of savage heat straight onto the cables. They twisted wildly, smoked, and then snapped one after the other. The burning ends were left depending from the underside of the lamp, and the cables from the roof were tumbling downwards, wrapping themselves round the latticed metalwork as they went.

Abna hardly waited to see these things. He dived immediately for the hovering plane, and with Viona and Mexone to help him he struggled into the cabin doorway, through it, and back into the control room.

"Quick," he ordered. "The Ultra."

The Amazon did not need to be told. Even as Abna closed the cabin door she was sending the 'plane sweeping upwards, and as she did so that she caught a glimpse of a group of overalled men rushing from the powerhouse below the tower and staring upwards.

"They're on to us," the Amazon said, as Abna, Viona, and Mexone gazed too. "Hardly to be wondered at. Severing these wires must have been immediately detectable in the building below—our only chance now is speed."

She put on the power to the best of her ability, but even so the speed was no greater than eighty miles an hour. As yet she had not solved the mysteries of the 'plane's control system sufficiently to understand how to apply the curious 'overdrive' mechanism and achieve the bullet velocity of which the craft was really capable. Even at eighty miles an hour the craft seemed to be crawling, and the Ultra, at a distance of perhaps twenty-five or thirty miles distance seemed to come nearer only very slowly.

"Say, take a look!" Viona exclaimed in sudden dismay. "To the rear!"

The others turned and looked through the window set in the tail of the craft. The vision was not reassuring. Half a dozen of the queer, wingless planes were streaking at an incredible speed across the sky, coming from the direction of the city.

"They're after us," the Amazon said. "Either the men in the tower powerhouse have told what's happened to the cables, or else we've been spotted as behaving oddly."

"Can't you get any more speed out of this thing?" Abna demanded anxiously. "We're just standing still compared to these pursuers."

"I'm doing the best I can."

The Amazon turned back to the controls and tried once again to figure out the overdrive system—but before she had got properly settled there came a jolt of the entire vessel as the first of the invading machines turned on some type of ray equipment.

"Try evasion," Abna said curtly, watching the pursuing fliers swarming round like wasps. "We can't make it direct to the Ultra. There just isn't time. Turn to one side—do anything!"

With that he turned to the plane's defensive weapons, Viona and Mexone at his side. But here again there was the problem of unfamiliarity, the struggle to understand the workings of guns and jets of which they had no prior knowledge. They just couldn't do it, for all their intelligence.

Meanwhile, the Amazon was trying every trick she could devise to avoid trouble. She set the machine darting, twisting, banking, looping—all the time getting further and further away from the treasured goal of the Ultra, all the time dodging the occasional blasts of rays and guns from the attackers—all the time coming nearer to the city from which they had fled with such difficulty.

Then finally there came a moment when the Amazon could dodge no longer. An aircraft was in front of her, and another not so very far behind. Helplessly she tried to twist from between them—

and failed. Both machines jetted rays at the same moment, and within the control room of the Crusaders' 'plane the roof suddenly split and the shatter-proof windows crushed themselves into powder and flew out of the frames.

Something must also have happened to the 'plane's exterior for the Amazon found it impossible to keep control over it any longer. Even as she juggled the controls violently up and down the machine fell into a steep dive and went down like a plummet, straight down, towards the tops of mighty buildings jutting out of the city.

"This looks like the finish!" Abna gasped, looking about him in vain for some signs of a parachute or safety device. "Nothing you can do?"

"Nothing!" The Amazon pulled frantically on the controls. "It's out of hand—"

She stopped her unavailing efforts as she realized how useless they were. In numb horror she and those grouped around her stared through the window as the roofs of the buildings swept up to meet them—then they struck edgewise against a beacon tower, probably for aircraft, perched on one of the taller buildings. The metalwork of the tower tore through the wall of the plane, but at least it stopped it falling. It hung almost upside down, caught on the tower like a kite on a telegraph wire.

The shock was colossal. All four Crusaders were hurled backwards to the furthest reaches of the control room and ended up in a smother of arms, bodies, and legs. Yet none of them was knocked unconscious even though they were badly bruised. Bit by bit they extricated themselves and stood with difficulty on the crazily tilted floor.

"Well, we're still in one piece, thank heaven," Abna commented at length. "And we're fortunate that these 'planes use magnetic force: there's no fuel to catch fire... We'd better get out," he added, forcing open the cabin door which was now in the 'floor.'

It squeaked under his efforts but finally jerked open. He stood on the edge of the doorway and looked into the abysmal spaces below, spaces that were now partly in deepening shadows as the night began to suddenly close in without the usual intervention of twilight.

The Amazon joined Abna at the doorway. She looked below, then above. Intently she watched the wheeling 'planes that were responsible for the present disaster. They milled around for a while like angry vultures, but they made no effort to descend into those canyons of streets between the buildings. Accordingly they turned and sped away across the darkening city.

"That may be a good sign—and it may be a bad one," the Amazon said, realizing Abna had been watching too. "Perhaps they've accepted the fact that we've been killed, or they're going to head for a more convenient landing space and then they'll come and investigate. Whichever it is we've got to move."

"And quickly," Abna agreed. "All right, we—"

He paused for a moment as the rapidly growing darkness was suddenly mitigated by the lights of the city. They sprang into being in all directions at once—beacon towers, windows and streets, transforming the whole gloomy picture into one of fairyland brightness.

"Night certainly comes quickly on this planet," the Amazon commented. "It may be a help to us. Let's get to the ground and see if we can somehow reach the Ultra."

She did not waste any further time on words but climbed out of the wrecked, crazily tilted 'plane and then got a firm hold on the tower's metalwork. Steadily she began to descend with the others a foot or two above her. Without mishap they reached the roof, but they glanced warily about them in readiness for any attack. All of them realized that surely the inhabitants of this building must have heard or felt the impact of the 'plane when it collided with the tower, and if they were normal they would come to investigate—

"There's an escape ladder there," Viona said, pointing to its curved top against the parapet of the roof.

The four began to move towards it and then paused and looked over their shoulders, studying a group of men who were emerging from a distant trapdoor onto the flat roof. So far they had not seen the quartet in the uncertain light: their attention seemed to be mainly directed towards the shattered 'plane hooked on the beacon tower.

"Quick—the ladder!" the Amazon said abruptly. "We can just dodge them—"

Successfully, as it happened. Swiftly the four slid over the parapet one after the other, still unobserved by the distant men who had emerged from below—then out of sight from those on the roof the four went swiftly and silently down the side of the building, dropping finally to a narrow street. Here they looked about them, not at all happy about the blaze of illumination around them, or the vision of colossal buildings on every side, their windows ablaze with the glow of industry—and, perhaps, the comforts of home.

"The Ultra's that way," Abna said, who had been studying a small compass always tuned to be in sympathy with the spaceship's magnetic prow. "We'll have to try and reach it somehow, particularly before they restore the nullifying influence on that tower we visited."

They began moving, always following the compass Abna held in his hand. They traversed brightly-lit ways and gloomily dark narrow ones, moving as well as they could through the more deserted regions of the city—but it was the kind of luck that could not hold forever. It deserted them when, apparently, the city workers left their duties at the sound of a shrieking siren. All at once as it seemed the formerly deserted ways became infested with men and women of all ages and variously dressed, hurrying in different directions, in exactly the same manner as the men and women of an Earthly city when work dissolved into the rush hour for home.

The Crusaders, crouched into a narrow doorway, watched the scene with misgivings. Men, women, and vehicles seemed to be everywhere. The crisis came when a vehicle, held up in the rush, stopped alongside them. It was something like an automobile, but used perhaps magnetic force for its propulsion since the controls were limited to a series of shiny buttons. Inside the dimly lighted cabin sat a solitary girl—fair-haired and not altogether unattractive.

The Amazon studied her, and the girl herself was too intently watching the traffic ahead to pay any attention to either side of her.

"Abna, give me that gun, of Rijilon's" the Amazon ordered abruptly. "Maybe this is a chance— Anyway, we're going to take it."

Abna handed it over. "You're not going to kill that girl, are you?"

"Of course not. I'm going to use her as an escort."

The Amazon moved forward, hidden from everybody else by the bulk of the vehicle. She pushed her head and shoulders through the open window and leveled the gun. Instantly the girl-driver looked sideways, an expression of blank terror coming to her face. The Amazon gave her a reassuring smile, reached inside the door, and snapped back the catch—then with a motion to the others she climbed into the automobile's surprisingly roomy interior.

The girl at the controls watched everything in fixed amazement. Her terror seemed to have subsided, but she was obviously sorely puzzled. Crouched behind her, the Amazon switched off the light in the roof and then said a few words.

"Keep going… Finish your journey." She knew she would not be understood but she emphasized her meaning with movements of the gun. To a certain extent the girl seemed to understand what she had to do: for the moment the traffic cleared she set the vehicle speeding forward.

"Abna, keep your compass checked," the Amazon said, "This girl's going to take us to the Ultra, even though she doesn't know it. Which way now?"

Abna peered at the compass' illuminated dial. "Bear left, then we'll be on a straight course."

The Amazon moved her gun upwards and indicated a leftward direction with the barrel. The girl glanced at the weapon within a foot of her face, then apparently understanding the direction that had been given she moved leftwards out of the traffic into a less busy and more dimly lighted side street.

"Okay now," Abna said. "Straight on."

Again the Amazon signified direction by means of the gun barrel. The girl nodded her fair head hastily in acknowledgement and kept on driving directly forward between the looming walls of buildings. Then through a park-like area, across a high river bridge, and onwards again into less busy regions.

"We're still on the right track," Abna commented. "We'll—"

He stopped suddenly as the automobile jolted. The girl had suddenly applied the brakes, and with one hand she indicated a party of uniformed men some distance ahead, under a hastily-erected spotlight. For the first time she spoke, in a hurry of musical but quite unintelligible words."

"Road block," the Amazon said, studying the scene. "Our escape's been discovered and the police, or whatever they are, are in action. This is going to be difficult—"

She had reckoned without the girl driver. Suddenly she seemed to come to a decision. From braking she changed to a tremendous acceleration, and at top speed hurtled the vehicle straight towards the group of men under the spotlight. There was a momentary vision of them, with raised hands, then they scattered for their lives as the girl tore through the midst of them and went hurtling on down the road, She was actually smiling now, as though she were enjoying herself.

"Good work," the Amazon told her, smiling at her reassuringly to make up for words that she knew would not be understood. "You're one after our own heart."

The girl gave a quick glance over her shoulder, which was sufficient for her to see the demoralized guards moving in all directions for their own vehicles—then she suddenly swerved to the left and shot down a side street. Another frantic burst of speed, left again, and then right. The vehicle was now in the midst of suburban regions and row after row of low-built buildings, which for all their peculiar design were probably houses—or, more correctly, bungalows. Whatever they were, the girl finally pulled up outside one of them with a shriek of brakes... Then she turned and looked at the Amazon urgently, pointing through the window at the same time.

CHAPTER 4

New Crusader

"It looks as though she wants us to get out of the car and go into the house," Abna said, as the Amazon crouched and frowned over the girl's movements.

"That'll be a risk," Mexone objected—and at that Viona looked at him.

"Why should it be? This girl's shown she's willing to help by the way she dodged those guards. We'll have a better chance of dealing with them in the house than we will here, if they catch up. I'd say take a chance."

"All right—we will," the Amazon said, and opening the door she clambered out into the roadway.

The others were only a moment following her example; then the girl came after them, indicating the house as she moved. She went quickly up the short front pathway, opened the door with an odd-looking key, and finally led the way into a living room. It was already lighted and the Crusaders followed her slowly, not at all sure what they were getting into. On the threshold of the doorway they paused, astonished by the remarkably homely and natural scene that met their eyes.

The room was comfortably furnished on an Earthly style, and indirectly lighted. Seated in comfortable chairs, in the midst of reading very thin metal foil sheets covered in ciphers—which were presumably the newspapers of this world—were a man and a woman in unusual but casual clothes. Plainly they were the girl's mother and father: she resembled both of them in many ways... So much the Crusaders had time to notice, in a matter of seconds perhaps, then the girl burst in her voluble speech, pointing to the quartet as they stood hesitating in the doorway. The mother and father listened in a kind of horrified astonishment, glancing at the quartet ever and again as the girl went on explaining.

Finally the Amazon went forward, and as a gesture of friendship she put Rijilon's gun in her golden belt and smiled a greeting. She spoke a few words, even though she knew the uselessness of them.

"We mean you no harm and are extremely grateful to your daughter for the help she has given us. I am the Golden Amazon,"— the Amazon pointed to herself and rep[eated her name—"and these are Abna, Viona, and Mexone. We are Crusaders. Crusaders."

The man repeated the word and then looked at his wife and daughter. The daughter was making urgent movements, obviously exasperated by the difficulty of language. Now she could be seen in the bright light she was revealed as a good-looking girl with gray eyes and a faintly mischievous expression—in fact very much like her opposite number: a teenager of Earth.

"We want to—" the Amazon started to say: then she swung sharply as there came a roar of power outside, followed by a savage hammering on the outer door.

"They've caught up," Abna said grimly. "This looks like trouble for these folks."

It was plain the teenage girl did not know what to do—and neither did her parents. Finally the Amazon made up their minds for them. She motioned for the girl to open the door, then glanced at Abna, Viona and Mexone.

"Let our friends come in here, then we'll deal with them," she said, moving to a position behind the room door.

The teenage girl waited until they were ready, then she strode through and unlocked the outer door. Almost immediately she was back in the room, hustled before the iron grip of the uniformed guards. As one forced the girl ahead of him, he talked, harshly and imperiously, obviously demanding information. He came within range of the watching Crusaders finally and the Amazon gave a cold grin. She moved forward silently—and the guard heard the slight movement and swung.

Instantly the Amazon's right fist lashed out. Remembering the iron strength of the men she'd encountered so far she made allowances and gave her uppercut everything it had got. The effect was astonishing: the guard's head jerked back as though it was on a hinge and he slewed round helplessly against the table and then crashed to the floor to lie motionless.

"Easier than I thought," the Amazon commented, rubbing her faintly tingling knuckles. "Perhaps he isn't so tough as the others we encountered."

"And what good does this do?" Abna demanded. "There must be others outside."

"Very probably. What it's done is to show these good people that we're friendly with them and not with the police or whatever they are." She looked towards the teenage girl and her parents as they stood watching in amazement; then she added, "If there are more outside maybe it's time they heard from us."

With that she sped into the small hallway, Rijilon's gun ready in her hand. Out in the street she beheld, from the doorway of the house, a curious type of vehicle behind the girl's deserted one—a vehicle containing four more men including the driver.

"Ready for a clean up?" the Amazon asked, as Abna, Viona, and Mexone came to her side. "It's possible that up to now these are the only men who know we're here. There'll be more comfort for everybody if we dispose of them."

"Let's go," Abna murmured.

They moved quickly down the pathway, but fast though they were the lights of the street picked them up and alerted the four men in the police vehicle to action. The driver was the first to have his gun leveled, but the Amazon saw his movement and fired the gun in her hand. It made a faint click, showed no sign of a report—and yet it crumpled the driver before he could make another move. Whatever the power in these strange guns it was certainly very efficient.

As for the other three men they didn't stand a chance at the hands of Viona, Abna, and Mexone. They were torn from their seats in the vehicle, their guns were whipped from them, then they sank down into unconsciousness before the rain of merciless blows that descended upon them. Unlike the earlier guards they were just strong men and, as such, easy game for the Crusaders. They had nothing of the superhuman strength of Iben Drass's particular followers.

"Three knocked out and one killed," Abna summed up. "What do we do with them?"

"Might take them into the house for the moment. We can't leave them here. Besides there may be neighbors around here who'll be wondering what's going on."

She put her gun away, and Viona, Mexone and Abna rejoined the other guards of theirs—then each with a guard slung over their shoulders the four returned into the house and looked at the girl and her parents inquiringly. The quick-witted teenager seemed to be the first to grasp the point for she opened a door that seemed to lead into a cellar. One by one the men were tumbled into it, including the guard who lay on the living room floor—then the door was closed and locked.

"So far, so good," the Amazon commented. "You others stay here with these three, I'm going to drive that squad car thing out of the avenue to avoid drawing suspicion on ourselves."

She went out actively and Abna turned to the three who were still watching in vast uncertainty. He motioned them to be seated, and then glanced at Viona and Mexone.

"We can't leave these good people without explaining what we're doing, or without thanking this girl for the risk she took to get us this far—yet every moment we're away from the Ultra the more chance there is of repairing that nullifying tower... The major difficulty is not having a language we can both understand."

Silence. Mexone and Viona nodded worriedly and the three of another world sat in uncomfortable silence as though expecting a major disaster any moment... Then the Amazon reappeared, which broke the tension somewhat. Under one arm she was carrying a small box.

"What's that?" Abna asked curiously, and as she dumped it on the table and flung back the lid she replied:

"I'm not certain, but I think it's a language translator on a small scale. It was in the squad car when I came to examine it."

"What did you do with the car? Viona asked.

"I took a short cut and found myself at the edge of a river. The squad car's now in it... Yes," the Amazon broke off, examining the instrument she had brought back with her. "I was right. It *is* a language translator of the portable transistor type. The very thing we need. Perhaps they're a sort of generally used piece of equipment on this planet. Anyway, here goes."

In a very short time she had figured out the instrument's major details. This done she took the suckered cables and fixed them on her forehead as she had seen Rijilon do it; then she went over to the teenage girl and looked at her inquiringly. Only for a moment did the girl seem to hesitate, then evidently sensing that nothing hurtful was intended she sat passive as the Amazon fitted the corresponding cables to her brow.

"Now," the Amazon said, "we can perhaps understand each other. Are my words making sense?"

A look of delighted surprise came to the girl's young voice, and she responded instantly in her own language. To the Amazon, the interpretation was flawless.

"Your words make complete sense to me."

"Good." The Amazon inspected the apparatus again, plugged a wire to what she assumed was an extension output, and then said:

"What is your name? And are these your parents?"

"I am named Thania, and these are my parents—yes." This time the girl's interpreted voice came clearly also through the loudspeaker attachment and Viona, Abna, and Mexone listened attentively.

"We have not a great deal of time to spare," the Amazon said, "but at least we can thank you for helping us. I should explain, who we are. I am the Golden Amazon, and this is my husband Abna. Our daughter Viona, and her husband Mexone. We come from a region of space unimaginably far away, and our purpose in space travel is to help those worlds which seem to need it... "

"And you believe this world of ours needs help?"

"Not this world—the world of Zon, to which we went before we came here. We have reason to believe that this world is unfriendly towards Zon and has plunged its people into a state of living death. We feel it is our duty to free them, but since coming here—for reasons too numerous to explain—we have run into hostility, particularly from an individual known as Rijilon."

"Rijilon," the girl said, "is the aide-in-chief to the President. And the President is the ruler of our—er—community. I—"

She broke off as she saw her father was making urgent signals. Finally she pulled the suckered cables from her forehead and handed them over. Her father fitted them into position and took up the story from his own angle.

"Whatever you have done, or are going to do, Golden Amazon, is not really any concern of ours, and it's more than our life's worth to fall foul of the law. We are a quiet, progressive people, and most of us are happy and comfortable, so much so that even our jails are nearly empty. Only very rarely do hostile members come amongst us—such as yourselves, and it is against such people that the law is continually alert. They come usually from one or other of the neighbor planets, hence the need for language translators since they speak a different tongue to ourselves."

"You make a mistake in regarding us as hostile," the Amazon said quietly. "We're only trying to help the world of Zon."

"The world of Zon doesn't require help—and all of you are fools if you try to give it any. Obviously it is because of your intention to help Zon that you have fallen foul of the law on this planet…"

"I assume Zon shouldn't be helped because you people on this world prefer to keep it in paralyzed subjection?" the Amazon demanded.

"That is correct… You have done little to endear yourselves here, Amazon. You waylaid my daughter as she came from her work—you forced her too take dangerous risks to avoid the law, and now you have actually put unconscious or dead guards in our basement. When the law catches up we'll be endangered for aiding and abetting you… Go—I beg of you, and be rid of these bodies that you have left here. Leave us in peace."

"Your daughter," the Amazon said, after thinking for a moment, "was not averse to helping us when she saw the law ahead."

"Thania is a self-willed girl. She knew she'd be caught with you had you stopped at that roadblock: that was why she took the fantastic risk of bringing you here. In any case, with a gun pointing at her head she could not do much else."

Thania herself, who had been registering growing indignation as she listened to the loudspeaker translation, finally signaled urgently to her father and transferred the suckered cables back to herself. Her young voice came forth urgently and excitedly.

"Father and mother have old and prosaic ideas, Amazon. They're not like me: they can't appreciate that I love excitement, danger and thrills. I enjoyed every minute of helping you, even though I didn't know what you really wanted. I felt sure somehow you didn't mean to harm me. I could sort of read it in your eyes—and in—er—Viona's."

Viona started and pointed to herself. "Me?"

"Why not?" Thania chattered on. "You're not much older than me, and oh how I envy you—cruising space and doing things to help people. I've space traveled, of course, because it's a normal thing on this world, but I've never been much further than the neighbor worlds. You must have wonderful adventures. So much more interesting than being a third rate clerk in a government office, like I am. The biggest thrill I ever got was buying that magnetic car of mine... But you four! What a wonderful life you must have!"

"At times it's a bit hair-raising," the Amazon said dryly. "However, be that as it may we ought to be moving. We have our spaceship to recover and then we'll—"

She stopped abruptly as she saw an expression of frozen horror come to Thania's face. She was gazing at a doorway behind the Amazon, so fixedly that the four Crusaders turned—and found themselves looking at Rijilon, as resplendent as ever, two iron-faced guards with leveled guns behind him. He smiled pleasantly enough, though there was a sting in his eyes. Stepping forward he snatched the suckered cables from Thania's forehead and clamped them on his own. Then his cultured voice came through the loudspeaker.

"Fortunate that we have traced you, my friends. I expected a longer search than this."

"Would I be speaking out of turn if I asked how you did it?" the Amazon inquired, and Rijilon gave her an amused glance.

"Not at all. I was rescued from the prison cell into which you so adroitly pushed me, and the rest of my information came from the headquarters on the watch for you. You had been traced this far, and I accompanied the remainder by heliplane. Hence my silent arrival.... A pity your efforts haven't been more rewarding. Naturally we shall resume where we left off. It is the order of the President—an order which I never had time to explain to you before you overpowered me—that you die, That order still stands."

Suddenly the girl Thania burst into a torrent of words, her face coloring with the fury of her emotions. Rijilon listened to her in impassive calm, then when at last she relaxed he answered her—and of course the translation came through the loudspeaker.

"Why exactly you should think it necessary to support these Crusaders in what they are doing escapes me, young woman. The fact remains that you and your parents have transgressed the law by giving sanctuary to these prisoners. You seem to regard them as gods, or something, because they lead a life to which you are unaccustomed—"

Again the volley of words, and evidently they must have contained something which was insulting to Rijilon's position for one of the guards abruptly stepped forward and with a single blow felled the girl to the floor. She collapsed whimpering, covering her head with her hands against further blows.

That did it, as far as Viona was concerned. She had conceived more than a liking for the fresh, bright-eyed teenager of another world, and seeing her ill-treated by the square brute of a guard was more than she could stand. Being the nearest to him she slammed her right fiat out abruptly, straight to his jaw. It was like hitting a concrete wall, and violent though the blow was he did little more than stagger—then Viona found herself in the man's irresistible grip, her arms being twisted up behind her with brutal force.

"Right," the Amazon murmured, clenching her fist. "Let them have it!"

She went into action instantly, regardless of the guns and the nearness of death. In one movement she knocked Rijilon off his feet, the sucker-cables pulling free of his forehead. Then she whirled up her right fist and brought it down with killing impact on the back of the guard's neck as he struggled with sadistic pleasure to break Viona's arms.

The blow, sufficient to break any ordinary man's neck, only distracted him for a moment, but even that one moment was enough for Viona for she managed to tear herself free. Then she turned to help her mother in battering the guard relentlessly, the gun torn out of his fingers.

In a matter of moments the whole fracas became a free-for-all, in which Thania and her parents joined in, more for the sake of perhaps getting free of the law for the time being than anything else. The girl and her parents lashed out right and left, dealing with the two guards and Rijilon himself, though compared to the mighty strength of the Crusaders their efforts were only those of babies.

The Amazon and Abna dealt with one guard, and Viona and Mexone with the other. Even so they had a tremendous struggle, for the strength and resilience of the two men was unbelievable. Rijilon, a more 'normal' proposition, was the prey of the girl and her parents, but he was more than a match for them. He swept Thania out of the way and dived for his gun. As Thania's parents made an effort to grab him he swung and fired quickly.

No smoke, no noise...but both man and woman slid slowly to the floor and became still. Thania, struggling to her feet, looked at them in helpless despair. A second later the Amazon had leapt forward, gripped Rijilon's wrist, and twisted the gun out of his hand. The remaining two guards, weakened at last by the crushing frequency of blows they kept receiving, slid to the floor and ceased to resist. They were not unconscious but they were certainly incapable of taking any more punishment.

From Thania there suddenly burst one of those torrents of words: clearly they were a mixture of grief and fury. She went over to her parents, clawing at them helplessly, then as there was no response from them she leapt to her feet and flung herself on Rijilon—or at least she intended to do so but Abna moved forward and restrained her, forcing her to calm down.

"Viona," the Amazon said, "see if Thania's parents are dead."

Viona obeyed. Then she looked up and shrugged. "They seem to be. I can't detect any heart or pulse beat."

The Amazon looked at the grim-faced Rijilon. Then she stooped and picked up the fallen cables of the language machine. In a moment she had established contact between herself and Rijilon once more.

"That," Rijilon said, before the Amazon had a chance to speak, "was not intended. I only intended to inflict wounds, to show them they could not flout authority—"

"Whatever you intended, they are dead," the Amazon snapped. "I can understand you wishing me dead—and my companions—but not a couple of middle-aged people of your own race. Somehow, you never struck me as that kind of man, Rijilon. Anyway, you are going to be useful to us. Under your authority we're going back to the Ultra, and it's up to you to see that we are not molested. If we are I'll kill you on the spot. I'll consider myself justified in doing that after what you've done to Thania's parents."

Rijilon did not respond but his mouth set harshly. He looked towards the two guards on the floor, both of them making no attempt to get up. Any help from that direction, as far as he was concerned, was obviously out. Then he gave a gasp as the Amazon ruthlessly whipped the sucker disks from his forehead and gave them to Thania. Sniffing back her tears the girl fixed them in position.

"Listen to me, Thania," the Amazon said quietly. "Your mother and father are dead. I don't want to sound brutal about it, but that is a fact. And you're not in a particularly safe position, either. Once we have gone the law will catch up with you and you'll be lucky if you escape with your life. You realize that?"

"Of course I realize it," Thania muttered, nearly too grief stricken to speak.

The Amazon continued: "Indirectly, we have brought all the tragedy and trouble on you—something we never intended. So there's only one answer, in order make sure of your safety. You must come with us."

Thania gave a start. She stared in amazement. "Come—come with you? Be a Crusader, do you mean?"

The Amazon smiled faintly. "Possibly even that could be done but that isn't our concern at the moment. I'm thinking of your safety. We're going back to the Ultra now, and Rijilon here will be forced to be our guarantee of safety... Now what is your answer?"

Thania did not hesitate for long. Her tear-filled gray eyes became suddenly eager.

"Yes, I'll do it, and be glad to. It would be even more wonderful if only mother and father... " Her voice broke as grief took over again. Abna tightened his grip upon her with paternal affection.

"Put these guards in the basement with the others," the Amazon said, glancing at Viona and Mexone. "They can fight it out for themselves."

Under the threat of the guns the guards had to obey. Evidently the guards already in the basement were not yet recovered, for there were no sounds from them. The Amazon watched the basement door close and Abna snapped the lock into place—then she took the sucker cables from Thania and put them back on Rijilon's forehead. In cold silence he listened to what she had to say.

"Go in the direction I shall indicate. We're going to use that heliplane of yours. If when we get to the Ultra, there are any signs of guard about you will dismiss them under any pretext you care to mention. I'm just warning you, Rijilon: don't make a single wrong move or it will be the worse for you. As you have heard, the girl Thania is coming with us. Understand?"

"May I ask if you are intending to carry on with your original plan once you've reached the Ultra? Flying to Zon with a piece of stone?"

"That is the plan," the Amazon agreed, at which Rijilon's urbane manner suddenly changed to obvious anxiety.

"I beg of you not to do it, Amazon, I beg of you—"

Rijilon went on talking in his own tongue, but it meant nothing, since the Amazon had wrenched away the cables. She folded the instrument in the box and slammed the lid.

"We'll take this with is: it may be useful," she said. "I'm going to leave it to you, Abna, to check the course as before. We'd better be off before worse things befall us."

She glanced towards the basement door from which there came a thunderous hammering as the guards evidently made up their minds to try and escape—then she led the way outside, the language instrument in one hand, and her gun in the other, pressed firmly in Rijilon's back.

One by one they boarded the heliplane, which was in the street, red lights around its body giving warning of its presence. Abna, at the Amazon's side, made a comment:

"Evidently 'planes in the street aren't considered unusual, if they're official ones."

The Amazon nodded and climbed into the control cabin. The others came quickly after her as she waved Rijilon to the machine's driving seat. Although she had had experience by now of piloting one of these machines she preferred to leave it to an expert.

"Which direction, Abna?" she asked, as Mexone closed the cabin door.

"Due south—straight ahead." Abna studied the compass in his hand.

The Amazon nodded, tapped Rijilon on the shoulder, and by hand signs indicated an upward movement—then a straight course. With a grim face the aide switched on the magnetic controls and the 'plane rose slowly from the street; then when it was at a height sufficient to clear the building tops it began to advance through the darkness, keeping on course as Abna gave directions and the Amazon relayed them by pantomime. And, gradually, the brightly lighted mass of the city was left behind, and there loomed ahead the dark regions of the surrounding land.

The journey to the Ultra was only a short one, and to the surprise of those within the 'plane, except Rijilon, the spaceship was picked out clearly in blazing arc-lights, whilst around it there stood a party of guards, gazing upwards at the moment towards the slowly descending heliplane.

"Looks as though we've got a reception committee," Abna commented.

"Evidently," the Amazon agreed. "Only to be expected, I suppose, after we wrecked that nullifying tower. The guards would know we'd head for the Ultra at the earliest moment. This is where our friend Rijilon will be useful."

She waited until the aide had brought the machine down within a few yards of the Ultra, then she quickly unfastened the lid on the portable language translator and fixed the cables to his head, and her own.

She said: "Here are your orders, Rijilon. "Tell those guards that we have been captured and that they can now dismiss. Get rid of them as quickly as possible. Thania here will know what you say."

"Very well, Amazon, I'll do that. But cannot I not ask you again not to attempt doing anything with Zon. It's vitally important that you shouldn't."

"I daresay it is—to you," the Amazon agreed; then she snapped, "Our plans are laid and we're going through with them. Now get busy."

She wrenched away the instrument cables, repacked it, and then waited. She and the others pressed well back out of sight of the cabin doorway as Rijilon unlocked it. As the door opened there was a vision of the guards outside in the portable arc-lights. What Rijilon said to them was unintelligible, but judging from the expression on Thania's dimly visible face he didn't attempt any trickery. And presently, the guards began to drift away, uncoupling the arc-lights and taking them to waiting vehicles not very far away. The Amazon crept forward and watched the scene of movement in the dim starlight, until finally the last vehicle had departed over the rough land towards the distant city.

Only then she did signal the others outside. They moved at once and joined her outside the heliplane. The only one who remained was Rijilon, still in the pilot's seat.

"You don't trust him?" Abna questioned, and the Amazon shook her head in the gloom.

"No. He's served his purpose and we'd never be able to trust him on board the Ultra. Let's move before he decides to use weapons against us."

Quickly they fled through the darkness, expecting but not receiving some sign of attack from the heliplane's weapons. Evidently Rijilon was content to let them escape, or else he felt that the darkness made his objectives uncertain.

The five reached the Ultra finally, Viona taking charge of the excited Thania. Abna led the way through the open airlock—still as it had been left—and into the great control room. He snapped the lighting switch over from battery to mains and to his delight illumination burst forth immediately.

"We're okay!" he exclaimed, swinging to the Amazon as she came in. "That nullifying tower hasn't been put back into service yet."

The Amazon hurried up the switchboard and breathed a sigh of thankfulness as the power plant instantly responded as she closed the switches. Finally she snapped the switch of the airlock door and watched it close. Then she glanced towards the central table on which there still reposed the chunk of rock exactly as Viona had put it there.

"That completes everything for the moment," the Amazon said. "We'd better depart—and then freshen up and have a meal."

CHAPTER 5

Revival

Once she was clear of the planet and the course set for 40-million mile distant Zon, the Amazon cut down the speed of the Ultra and relaxed for a while with the others. In any case there was no desperate hurry to reach the standstill planet now they had got what they wanted in the shape of a random element.

Washed, and refreshed with a good meal, all five felt better able to exchange confidences, and as far as Thania was concerned—now attired in one of Viona's spare black space uniforms—there was no difficulty in regard to speaking since the Language Translator was switched on, and would remain so until the girl had been given a good knowledge of English.

"All things considered," Abna said, "we did well to get away with that lot as we did, and I imagine the most discomfited person in the whole business will be Rijilon, who had promised the President we would be disposed of."

The Amazon looked thoughtful. "I can't quite understand Rijilon. He's a man of intelligence and courtesy, and yet he treated us as bitter enemies. Neither can I understand why he should be so anxious to stop us going to Zon and reviving it—except of course that it undoes all his work as far as paralyzing the planet is concerned. I assume he was responsible in the first place. Do you happen to know the facts, Thania?"

The girl shrugged. "I know very little of what takes place in the government of any planet, I'm afraid, though being in the government offices I do get to know more than most. I know there was a decision by the President to immobilize the world of Zon, and our scientists put it into effect. What they did I can't say."

"We know what they did," Abna said grimly, "but we're not at all sure *why* they did it. On the face of it, Thania, it looks as though the people of your planet constituted a danger to Zon, and because of that danger the people of Zon built a vast defensive system on their planet—only to be outwitted again as a paralysis descended upon them, engineered by Rijilon."

Thania looked thoughtful. "Somehow," she said, "I cannot imagine the people of my planet being a danger to anybody. They are a peaceful, progressive people—and so for that matter are the inhabitants of the other planets in the system. One or two groups of peoples on the other worlds are unpleasant sometimes but they're certainly not a danger. I confess I don't understand the mystery of Zon in the least: it's a matter that's only understood by the government."

"I think," the Amazon said slowly, "that as yet we have only touched the fringe of the problem regarding that planet. Some day we'll find out why that paralysis happened, and that can only come by reviving the people of Zon themselves and questioning them."

There was a brief silence. The Ultra flew on through the gulf, the hum of the atomic power plant the only thing disturbing the quiet. Thania looked dreamily towards the observation window, her young eyes full of a thousand thoughts as she studied the star-studded enigma of the Milky Way. Then presently she spoke:

"You said that perhaps I might become a Crusader: Did you really mean that, Amazon?"

The Amazon smiled. "Of course I meant it—providing you are prepared to undergo certain surgical transformations which will affect both your body and your mind. It will not be painful, but it may be against your wishes."

"Transformations?"

The Amazon nodded towards Mexone. "Originally, Mexone was much as you are, a young man who was dissatisfied with his own world, a young man, strong and healthy, who thought he'd enjoy our way of life. He became a Crusader, and he underwent the surgical transformation of which I speak. He can tell you his reaction from personal experience."

"My reaction has been only one of pleasure," Mexone shrugged. "All the operation does is transform natural strength into about five times the normal, with a corresponding increase in mental alertness."

"You mean change a normal person into a super being?"

"You might call it that," the Amazon agreed. "Your general physique is altered to give you the great strength necessary in the tasks we perform, and brain surgery links up certain areas of the brain that in the normal way are under used. The finished effect is, as you say, a super-being."

Thania's gray eyes were shining. "And was that your own experience, Amazon? Did you become a superwoman because of a surgical operation?"

"I did, my dear—but in my case I had no say in it. I was a baby when it happened. It was many years ago during a fantastic war on my home planet of Earth—" The Amazon checked herself. "But this has nothing to do with your case. Do you wish this surgery to be undertaken?"

"I do. Definitely I do. I want to become one of you and help in the wonderful things you do… After all, what is there for me now on my own planet? My parents dead, my own life in danger— Yes! Make me a Crusader."

The Amazon smiled at the girl's enthusiasm and got to her feet.

"Come with me, Thania. We can finish the operation and have you well on the way to recovery before we reach Zon. The surgical laboratory is in another portion of the ship."

Thania rose without hesitation. "In a way, I suppose your operative process is similar to that performed on all members of the Presidential guard."

The Amazon frowned. "What do you mean?"

"You've had experience of the guard, haven't you? You know the enormous strength they possess. That's the outcome of a kind of surgery they undergo when they join the Presidential Guard. It does not make the men any more intelligent, but it certainly gives them a terrific strength and resistance"

"Mmm, so that's the answer." The Amazon reflected for a moment. "A very good idea too, as far as the guards are concerned. I didn't notice Rijilon was particularly tough. A normal man, I'd say."

"Of course. He doesn't belong to the guard. He's an aide to the President. A sort of right hand man."

The Amazon said: "Once this operation is performed you will find yourself nearly the equal of one of the guards. Come with me."

Viona smiled as she watched them leave the control room, then she glanced at Abna and Mexone.

"I'm glad about this—really glad. I took a liking to Thania the moment I saw her. I think she'll make a good Crusader."

Abna nodded. "I think you're right. In any case I trust to your mother's judgment: she formed the Crusaders and in picking its members for them she's never been wrong in her judgment. She certainly wasn't wrong when she chose you, Mexone—the first of what I might call the outside members."

Mexone smiled. "I've never regretted the decision that led me to throw in my lot with you."

"In regard to Thania—" Ahna started to say, then he suddenly broke off and stared through the observation window. "Spaceships—and not far behind!" he exclaimed. "A complete fleet of them! It must be Rijilon pursuing us."

He had been moving to the window whilst speaking, and a brief silence fell as Mexone and Viona joined him. There was no doubt of the fact that a hundred or so space machines were streaking through the void in the rear of the slowly moving Ultra.

"Never a dull moment!" Viona murmured, cocking an eye on her father. "I wonder what they hope to accomplish against a ship like ours? We can blast them out of existence if we choose."

"Of which fact they must be well aware," Abna muttered. "Why then such suicidal tactics— I'd better have a word with your mother."

Turning, he hurried through the various corridors of the mighty vessel until he came to the laboratory. The Amazon was quietly working at the switchboard, controlling the automatic apparatus that was performing surgery on Thania, lying under anesthetic on one of the long tables.

"Anything wrong?" the Amazon asked, seeing Abna's expression.

"Not yet—but maybe there soon will be. Rijilon and a fleet of machines are on our tail. What do you suggest I do with them?"

The Amazon reflected. "My first retort to that is—destroy them! But I hesitate to do that unless we are attacked. There must be a very vital reason for them traveling after us, knowing as they must that the Ultra has a very destructive armory—"

"That's what Viona said: they're risking complete destruction."

"Unless I'm mistaken," the Amazon mused, "they're still worrying over our taking a piece of stone to Zon, and it must be a real worry indeed if they're risking a fleet to try and stop us. Try contacting them by radio and switch in the Language Translator to the circuit. That way they'll make sense to us, and we to them. We may as well see what they want."

"Right. I'll do that—"

"I'll be with you in about ten minutes," the Amazon added. "This surgical job will be done by then."

Abna hurried out and returned to the control room. As quickly as possible he connected the Language Translator to the radio equipment and then switched on, watching the perceptibly nearer fleet as he waited for the apparatus to link up. Finally he spoke:

"Abna speaking from the Ultra. Why are you pursuing us? Over."

There was a brief pause, then came the recognizable voice of Rijilon through the loudspeaker of the Language Translator:

"This is Rijilon speaking. I have new orders from the President that I am instructed to pass on to you. We are nearing Zon so there is little time to lose. Can you understand me? Over."

"I understand you perfectly," Abna answered, rather dryly. "If it'll make your President feel any happier I'll listen to what he has to say this time—but it can't make any difference to our plans regarding Zon. Over."

"The President is willing to overlook your behavior on our world and gives you complete pardon—including the girl Thania— If you wish to come to our planet and discuss scientific matters. But immunity from the death sentence originally imposed carries the proviso that you must avoid all contact with Zon. Over."

"Why do you bring a fleet to qualify a statement like that?" Abna demanded. "Over."

"I have brought a fleet of war machines to dissuade you by force from approaching Zon if you do not comply with the President's offer. Over."

Abna reflected for a moment and then replied: "You're just wasting your time, Rijilon. Over."

"At least restore the girl Thania to us! There's a vital reason why you should. Over."

"There's no reason at all," Abna retorted. "She's decided to throw in her lot with us and abandon her home planet. And that decision remains. You're wasting your time, Rijilon. Over and out."

Abna switched off the radio and restored the Language Translator in its normal status for when Thania should return. Then he moved to the window and stood surveying. The fleet was making no attempt to slow down or about turn: rather it was accelerating.

After a moment or two invisible rays came from the pursuing machines, making their presence felt by a series of violent impacts. Abna glanced at Viona and Mexone and gave a grim smile.

"Rather like ants attacking an elephant," he commented. "All right, if they want fun and games they shall have it." He glanced at the Ultra's deadly armory, and then shook his head. "No. Wholesale destruction is against our principles, unless we're fighting for our lives. Maybe there's a better way."

He turned to the switchboard, moved and operated the speed controls. He smiled as with a mighty surge the Ultra shot forward, leaving the fleet dropping away into space... Yet another increase in acceleration, and the Ultra was hurtling at an enormous velocity straight towards Zon as it loomed ahead. The fleet in the distance visibly put on speed, but to keep pace with the Ultra was impossible.

Abna turned at a sudden sound and the Amazon came into the control room. Beside her was Thania—a changed and smiling Thania, the teenage imperfections of her figure somehow straightened out and rounded, satin-like curves of iron strength had replaced them.

"Everything in order?" Abna asked, and both Thania and the Amazon nodded.

"The operation has been successfully completed," the Amazon said. "Here, Thania. Try your strength on this..." and she took an iron bar up from the tool bench and handed it over.

"You mean—?" Thania's gray eyes were wide in amazement.

"I mean bend it," the Amazon smiled. "You can now, you know."

It was obvious the girl did not believe it, but nevertheless she took the iron bar between her slender hands and made an abrupt effort. Nobody was more surprised than she when the bar bent like a warm candle.

"From now on consider yourself a Crusader," the Amazon said, patting her shoulder. "And we're glad to have you amongst us. Now, Abna, how did you make out with Rijilon? What did he want?"

Briefly Abna summed up the situation. The Amazon listened, meanwhile looking through the window upon the hurtling fleet in the distance. They were still pursuing, hopeless though they must have realized their task was. The Amazon frowned as she watched.

"I still say it's all very strange," she said at last. "The situation, for them, seems to be almost a desperate one: they've got to step us reaching Zon and reviving it, no matter what the cost. I wonder if we've got our facts wrong somewhere?"

"Wrong?" Abna echoed in surprise.

"Yes. We assume that reviving Zon is a necessity for the people of that planet, but we're not absolutely sure of that: it's entirely an assumption."

"And the correct one," Viona insisted. "Naturally, Rijilon and the President don't want Zon revived. They want it eliminated, so they're going all out to stop us undoing their work."

"If they want Zon eliminated why didn't they destroy everybody instead of paralyzing them?" the Amazon questioned, her violet eyes thoughtful. "I'm becoming uneasy about the whole thing. Rijilon seems to be so desperate to stop us."

Usually it was Abna who counseled caution, but this time he did not—surprisingly. He said bluntly:

"You're simply being swayed by Rijilon's persistence, Vi. We're going to follow out our plan as we made it."

The Amazon shrugged. "Very well—as you say. Maybe my instincts are playing me false."

So the journey to Zon continued at overwhelming speed. Rijilon's fleet was almost lost in the distance, even though it still pursued. Until finally the Ultra was cleaving through Zon's motionless air, sweeping down towards the spreading vastness of the paralyzed city. Thania surveyed the scene below in awe, fascinated by this first-hand view of a world she had only heard about up to now.

"And you intend to revive everything?" she asked, standing by the Amazon's side.

"That is our intention."

"With a piece of stone?" Thania's eyes strayed to it on the table. "I don't understand how such a thing is possible."

"It'd take too long to explain, Thania, even though you would quite understand me with the scientific knowledge which has been impregnated into your brain. Let's just say—"

The radio buzzed for attention. In surprise the five looked at it.

"It'll be Rijilon again," Abna said after a moment. "He'll have to buzz in vain."

He returned his attention to the control board, slowing down the Ultra's speed as swiftly as possible. Even so he had to circumnavigate Zon several times before he finally had slowed the great vessel down enough to permit of landing—and in that time Rijilon's fleet had caught up and were visible in a swarm just beyond the limits of the atmosphere. Even though the radio still buzzed for attention the five ignored it.

"Here we go," Abna said finally, and brought the vessel down in one of the park-like spaces. Then he snapped the switch that set the airlock opening ponderously.

The Amazon crossed to the table where lay the stone. She hesitated over picking it up and instead turned to the radio, which still insistently demanded attention. She switched it on, plugged in the Language Translator, and then spoke.

"You have had your answer from Abna, Rijilon, and there is nothing more to say. Over."

"But there is!" came Rijilon's urgent voice. "I beg of you not to disturb that world of Zon, Amazon—for the sake of the other worlds in the system. If you will consent to an audience I will explain in full, and I will see to it that all of you are pardoned for whatever happened earlier. I couldn't explain before because the President's orders did not permit of it. I would have said more, only Abna cut the contact. Over."

"I'm listening," the Amazon said quietly. "Why shouldn't we restore this world? Over."

"If you do so you will release from sleep the cruelest race ever known in any system of worlds, a race armed with engines of destruction mighty enough to shatter every world in the system. That was the avowed intention of the Zonians before we found a way to paralyze them. We could have killed them, but mass destruction is not the President's wish, so we decided on immobility produced by thermodynamic equilibrium. Over."

The Amazon watched Thania as she strayed to the open airlock and looked interestedly outside. Then she said:

"You mean... You mean that the numberless machines on this planet are really weapons of aggression, not defense? Over."

"That is exactly what I mean. Have you not examined them? Over."

"Not thoroughly enough to understand what they are. We

evidently jumped to the wrong conclusion… Over."

"We tried to eliminate you at first—not realizing that you were in ignorance of the true facts. Now we know differently we beg of you to confer with us again, on a different standing. But please leave Zon alone. Over."

The Amazon glanced at Abna and he slowly nodded. "Better do as he says. Looks as though we'll stir up a hornet's nest if we start throwing a stone in this thermodynamic pool—" He broke off and gave a start. "Great heavens, Thania! Look!"

The Amazon spoke briefly into the microphone. "Hold on a minute, Rijilon. Something's happened. I'll be back. Over and out."

Darting across the control room the Amazon came to Abna's side. He was staring out into the park-like space, across which Thania was walking, evidently intent on investigating for herself. There was nothing wrong in this, as such— The trouble lay in the things that were happening around her. Everywhere she moved the moss-like grass was losing its stiff appearance and little eddies of dust were commencing to arise. Even the atmosphere had a trace of movement, enough anyway to set the leaves of the branches moving.

"What's going on?" Viona asked curiously, coming over with Mexone and joining her mother and father in the airlock. "Things don't look so quiet around here as they did before."

"They're not," the Amazon replied curtly, "nor will they ever be again. We've done the very thing Rijilon was warning us against."

Viona stared. "Done it? But how? That stone's still on the table—"

"The stone doesn't signify anymore. Thania herself is as much a random element as the stone is, and unintentionally she's been the key that has unlocked this motionless prison. She's of a planet in this system and therefore of the right basic materials to provide a random element. We never thought of that. The fleet circling outside the atmosphere at this moment never comes to the planet itself, or even within its atmosphere, for fear of producing the very effect that Thania is producing now… We and the Ultra are all right, being of a different system entirely."

For a moment there was a horrified silence, but there was certainly no doubt that the Amazon was right. With every second disturbance was increasing—and would continue to do so—for with the extra energy of Thania's body to work on the shuffling of atoms could start again into a new pattern. It would be only a matter of hours before the disorganization would have affected every molecular pattern on the planet and restored it back to life.

"Thania!" the Amazon called suddenly. "Thania!"

At the sound of her name the girl turned, pointed to herself, and then obeyed the Amazon's signals to come back to the Ultra. She walked through the stirring grass and entered the control room smiling, apparently not in the least aware that she had done anything wrong.

"Keep your eye on her, Abna," the Amazon said, and hurried back to the radio equipment. She picked up the microphone. "Rijilon, are you receiving me? Over."

"Yes, Amazon—I am receiving you. Over."

"The unexpected has happened. We haven't thrown the stone upon Zon, but something even more alarming has happened. Thania herself stepped onto this world and at this moment it's showing signs of revival. Over."

"Leave it quickly," came Rijilon's urgent voice. "We will do all in our power to repair the damage. Come away! Join us, if you wish—otherwise fly away into space as far as you can go. Over."

"That we shall never do," the Amazon retorted. "We'll join you as fast as possible. Over and out."

She pulled out the contact with the Language Translator and restored it to normal, then she turned to Thania. By this time the girl had guessed that she was responsible for something unusual. She gave the Amazon a troubled glance.

"Have I done something I shouldn't, Amazon?"

"Yes—but quite unwittingly." The Amazon patted her arm and then hurried to the control board. "Walking on this planet as you did has restored it to life. Within a very short time it will be alive again and the people with it."

"But—but why? I don't understand."

The Amazon snapped the control switches and was silent for a few moments as the Ultra swept into the upper atmosphere, away from the writhing clouds and strange stirring movement below.

"To put it briefly," she sad, "you've become a random element. I'll explain to you..." and she gave the full scientific details. Thania listened in silence, her surgically sharpened brain capable of taking in the meaning of thermodynamic equilibrium, and the need for an outside source of energy to start again the process of shuffling and entropy.

"Then—then I unlocked that world, without knowing it?" she asked, her eyes wide.

"Correct—because you are a being born of this system's neighbor world which has an exactly similar constitution to Zon. Therefore the materials that make you up are exactly of the right type from which to exchange energy. Without going into the involved mechanics of thermodynamics that is the situation."

"I'm most dreadfully sorry, Amazon. I never realized... "

"No, Thania. How could you?" The Amazon patted her arm reassuringly. "It was just one of those things."

"Will my departure not cause the revival process to slow down and stop again? When I'm no longer there my energy can't be used, can it?"

"The process is involved, and hard to explain," the Amazon mused. "Let's say it's a sort of chain reaction, which you have started. I'm afraid your departure from the scene won't make any difference. Look below—even in this short time."

Thania did so—ad so did Abna, Viona, and Mexone. There was no doubt about the change that had come over the world of Zon. Apart from the cloud movement there was a wind, disturbing the green areas. And in the canyons of streets traffic was commencing to move and a myriad dots—living beings—were shifting and altering as they found life once again.

"Nothing we can do," the Amazon shrugged. "We'd better accept Rijilon's hospitality, such as it is—and see what he has in mind."

Though she had inward doubts about the man after having crossed swords with him she had nevertheless the inner conviction that he would keep his word about the amnesty the President had granted. Anyway, she was prepared to risk it—and with this in mind she turned the Ultra slightly in its course until its nose was heading towards Rijilon's fleet, still drifting in the distance. In a matter of minutes she was almost upon it; then she moved from the switchboard and plugged the Language Translator into the radio once more.

She switched on. "Rijilon? Amazon speaking. Come alongside and we'll anchor your airlock to ours, then you can join us. Over." Switching off the microphone for a moment she added to Abna, "If he comes here we'll feel safer until we're sure if he really means what he says."

"Wise precaution," Abna agreed.

Rijilon's voice came through the loudspeaker. "I am coming alongside as you have instructed, Amazon. Over and out."

The quintet watched as one space machine detached itself from the remainder of the fleet and moved swiftly into position. When at last it was alongside the Amazon switched on the magnetic grapples and the vessel was drawn flush against the Ultra's vast bulk. The airlock opened, and so did that of Rijilon's ship, leaving a clear corridor from one control room to the other.

While this was proceeding, Abna switched the Language Translator back to normal and then stood watching as the dignified Rijilon came slowly across from his own ship and inclined his head slightly as he saw the Amazon regarding him.

"I am grateful, Amazon, that you have decided to trust me," he said. "In all truth, I meant what I said on the radio. Now we are faced with a common danger—the revival of Zon. But you still have the opportunity to leave this system and abandon its troubles entirely."

"We never abandon trouble: we face it," the Amazon replied. "What exactly do you propose doing?"

The aide crossed to the window and meditated for a moment as he looked down on the reviving planet. Then he turned.

"I am not in a position to make my own decisions: that is the prerogative of the President. Speaking unofficially I should think that since we once paralyzed this planet we can do so again—and that's the suggestion I shall make to the President. We must return to my own world at once. Every second of delay makes the ultimate task harder."

"You can't explain fully what it's all about, I suppose?" Abna asked. "All we know is that Zon is a dangerous planet—a threat to your world and the others around it. Can't you elaborate a little?"

"I would not presume to do so without the President's sanction, Abna. Let us be on our way immediately. Might I use your radio, to inform my second-in-command of what we intend to do?"

"Pray do," the Amazon murmured, and with that odd little inclination of the head Rijilon moved to the instrument...

* * * *

It was some hours later when the Ultra and Rijilon's fleet at last touched down on his world—Karg, by name. And this time, as far as the Crusaders were concerned, it was a return in state compared to the snatch-and-depart effort of their earlier experiences.

Still with that same dignity, Rijilon conducted the five of them to an edifice in the city center—not a very long journey since they had landed at the city's official space and airport. Once within the building they were conducted down a series of passages lined with watchful guards, and ultimately into what were plainly the chambers of the President—one vast room, into which they stepped, with several anterooms leading from it.

And at a broad and very normal-looking desk was the President himself, a middle-aged man with graying hair, the most notable thing about him being his friendly smile. Here was no tyrannical personality but a man of obvious charm and gentility.

"The Golden Amazon and the Crusaders, sir," Rijilon said, when a voice translator had been switched on. "They decided to accept your offer of amnesty and have audience with you."

"Splendid," the President murmured. "And Zon? What has happened there?"

"The worst, sir, I'm afraid. The planet is reviving."

"So I understand. The telescopic division has just reported it to me. Our friends here deposited the stone as intended, then?"

"No," the Amazon put in. "That was brought about by a combination of most unfortunate circumstances which I'll explain later. For the moment your main concern should be—and probably is—to rectify the damage."

"True—but how? Have you any suggestions, Rijilon?"

"Only that we try the paralysis again before restoration gets too great a hold."

The President nodded. "Do that, then, and report progress to me. And do it at once."

Rijilon gave a salute and then departed. The President waved to chairs and then sat back, his blue eyes searching each Crusader in turn.

"I am afraid," he said finally, "that we meet under rather strained circumstances. Upon the first occasion when you arrived I issued orders for your death, mainly because I believed you were in league with Zon in some way or other and were determined to revive the inhabitants of that planet, no matter what."

"That was our original intention," the Amazon shrugged. "It was still our intention up to the time when Rijilon contacted us in space. Only then did we realize that there must be some vital reason for withholding our hand... But we have never been in league with the Zonians. We haven't even any idea what they are like, their form of government, or anything."

"They are the vultures of our five-world system," the President said bitterly.

"Why are they? Surely you of this world have ingenuity and science enough to hold them in check?"

"We had the ingenuity and science to paralyze them in their tracks before they could destroy us—a feat which we accomplished by taking them by surprise. Now you have undone all that work. Might I ask what happened exactly?"

The Amazon explained the circumstances. At the end of it the President sighed and his blue eyes moved to Thania. She averted her gaze and murmured an apology.

"It couldn't be helped," the Amazon said. "That's one reason why we'll try and help you to rectify the damage we've done, but we must know what we're fighting."

"You are fighting a race of people that have created an artificial world and are determined to clothe it in the vestments usually attributed to a planet—namely, air and water."

The Amazon frowned. "Created a world? Where? I haven't seen it."

"You won't have done so. It is of black, non-reflective metal, and exists about eighty million miles from Zon itself, outside our five-world system. The Zonians were just on the verge of completing their plans for this mechanical planet of theirs when we stopped them."

"Why should clothing this synthetic planet with air and water affect you?" Abna asked.

"It affects us because the air and water will be that of our own world, and the three more or less friendly neighbor worlds who are around us. It is the avowed intention of the Zonians—which fact we learned from our intelligence department—to strip every world around them of air and water and transplant it to their metal planet. I need hardly add that this would have a devastating effect on us, and if we try to resist they have science and weapons of an order far ahead of ours."

The Amazon said thoughtfully: "I begin to see what you arc up against. But the reason for this metal planet? How big is it? What do the Zonians want it for?"

"How big is it?" The President reflected. "About six times the size of Zon itself—a good deal bigger than all the planets in this system put together. A masterpiece of cosmic engineering and, so far as the intelligence department has been able to discover, they need the planet for two reasons—one to solve the problem of their own overcrowded population, and two, to use the planet as a scientific base and leaping off point for the deeps immediately beyond this system. What their final intentions are I don't know, but the immediate one is certainly to solve their overcrowding problem. Zon is an older planet than the others, and of course its civilization is more advanced and more congested because of it."

"And the idea is to clothe this world of theirs at the expense of the other planets?" the Amazon questioned. "I can understand them needing the resources of four planets, excluding their own, to clothe this metal world in air and water, but why did they go to the trouble of making a giant world? With the scientific ability they've got wouldn't they have found it easier to attack the planets in their own system, wipe out the populations, and take ever?"

"Certainly they could do it, but in the process they would lose untold members of their race, and there isn't one of them who isn't a useful scientist to the community. By whipping away air and water from their neighbor worlds they are safe from attack, or at least more so than they would be if they engaged in open warfare. Any of the four worlds including ours have science that could greatly reduce their numbers, and they don't intend to risk it… Now perhaps you can see the danger in reviving a planet like that?"

"Indeed I do," the Amazon assented. "From the very first moment we arrived on this planet, I somehow could not see any of you, from your Imperix to your aide, being ruthless killers. None of you had that stamp. You struck me as being a quietly intelligent race, but on the other hand—having no real knowledge of the situation—it looked as though it was Zon that needed help. Even more so did you seem to be the dangerous ones when you tried to kill us on Zon—and again later sentenced us to death."

The President smiled faintly. "We tried, when you were on Zon, to make you immobile, but since you are of a different constitution to ourselves the effort failed. We had the idea that, somehow, you were in league with Zon and therefore our enemies. It had been a chapter of cross-purposes from the very start... Which I hope we can now rectify."

"Agreed," the Amazon said, holding forth her yellow hand. "We understand each other now—we are engaged against a common foe."

CHAPTER 6

Commander Nio

It seemed that the President was on the verge of speaking again when an instrument on his desk whirred softly for attention. He snapped a switch and spoke. Instantly there came the familiar voice of Rijilon, his normal language translated immediately by the language machine. In silence the five Crusaders listened.

"We have made the first moves in an attempt to paralyze Zon, sir, but they have proved ineffective. The planet is now almost completely recovered and we have lost the former advantage of surprise. The Zonian scientists are prepared for anything we try to do and, so far, they have warded off our efforts to again produce paralysis. What are my orders?"

The President gave a worried frown and hesitated. Then before he could answer the Amazon leaned across towards him.

"Tell him to stop wasting his time. Maybe we can do something."

The President nodded and said into the instrument: "Attempt nothing further for the moment, Rijilon. I will give you fresh instructions when I've decided what has to be done."

"Yes, sir."

The President switched off and then looked up as the Amazon got to her feet. Automatically, the others rose too.

"Just what do you propose doing?" the President asked, and at that the Amazon shrugged.

"At the moment I'm not quite sure, but at least we can review the position in your laboratory with your scientists. Our science is apparently about level with yours, but we also have certain devices that are even ahead of you—and they may be for the Zonians. One weapon in particular, our Zero Thought Amplifier, could be used if everything else fails, but it is so vastly destructive and ruthless that we always hesitate to use it. There may be another way. For the moment we'd better confer with your laboratory technicians."

"By all means. I will have you conducted there immediately."

And within ten minutes the quintet were in the midst of the machines and instruments of the city's main laboratory—an enormous building in the center of the city, with myriads of adjoining laboratories and anterooms. In charge here was Railus, a small-built man with the typical look of a scientist. At the time when the Crusaders were conducted into his presence he was in the midst of consultation with Rijilon himself.

A language translator in operation the Amazon spoke:

"Our science is at your disposal, and I hope your science is at ours. Between us we might be able to do something. The immediate problem, as I see it, is that the attempt to produce a second paralysis has failed."

"Utterly," Railus said. "I'm afraid we have lost the initiative completely. Come and look for yourselves."

Turning, he led the way through the midst of the machines and armies of technicians into a large adjoining chamber. There was only one instrument in it, a huge assembly of girders and reflecting mirrors that reached to the lofty, domed roof. Plainly it was a telescopic reflector, a fact proven in a moment or two when the lights dimmed and upon a vast three dimensional wall screen there appeared a view of Zon itself, as if viewed from a few thousands of miles out in space.

Railus operated a series of switches and the view came a great deal closer, giving a hover-picture of the planet from about a thousand-foot altitude.

Because there was no language translator in the room Railus did not attempt to explain—and neither did Rijilon. In fact they had no need. The transmitted scenes were self-explanatory and the Crusaders studied them in grim silence. If ever a planet had come back to life this one had. Activity and industry were everywhere. People moving, vehicles traveling, aircraft sweeping through the skies. Chimneys were belching smoke from foundries, beacons on top of buildings were flashing continuously— In a word, a planet of seething activity where formerly there had been utter stagnation.

"And I caused all that," Thania sighed, and since she spoke in her own language Rijilon and Railus looked at her quickly. They did not comment, however, and the Crusaders wondered what she had said.

Finally Railus switched the scene off and led the way back into the laboratory where the language translator stood. The Amazon gave Thania a sharp glance and asked a question.

"What did you say in the observatory, Thania?"

"I said I caused all that. I'll never forgive myself."

"The sooner you stop brooding over your unintentional mistake, the better," the Amazon said. "Nothing's accomplished by it— And Viona, when you get the chance, you'd better start transferring a knowledge of the English language to Thania with the mechanical educator we have aboard the Ultra, then we'll understand each other better. Now, to the matter on hand— Railus, what is the immediate danger? Obviously Zon is completely restored, so what do you think the Zonians will do next?"

"You know of their plan to denude us and our neighbors of air and water? The President has told you?"

"Every detail."

"Then I think they will do that, since they were on the point of doing it when we paralyzed them. We don't know which world they'll strip first but I think it will be this one, in response for our rendering them powerless. They know it was our world which caused it—and it's natural to think they'll take reprisal and strip the neighbor worlds later."

The Amazon reflected. "You say they were on the point of doing it before? That means the machinery is all ready to go as far as they are concerned?"

"That seems a certainty," Rijilon said grimly. "At any moment disaster may strike us, and our science is not advanced enough to know how to offset the danger."

"It's a problem," the Amazon agreed, "but it might not be insurmountable. Protecting a planet is only a matter of working on a big scale. We have machines aboard the Ultra which protect it from all manner of dangers—maybe something can be done in a similar way to protect your world whilst we get a little breathing space..." The Amazon glanced about her. "Is there somewhere where we can confer in peace? These machines and technicians are a little distracting."

Railus motioned to an anteroom, carrying the language translator with him on its stand. Once within the office the Crusaders and men of Karg sat down at a table, dominated by the Amazon. From her tense, analytical manner she was obviously in the midst of deep scientific thought.

"To take air and water from this planet some kind of magnetic power will have to be used by the Zonians," she said, "and it is against that that you have to prepare. As I see it we need to do as we do on the Ultra—counteract the magnetism with repulsion. The matter of magnetism should not be difficult for you since you even fly your spaceships on magnetic lines of force."

"It would depend," Railus said thoughtfully, "upon the kind of magnetism which will be projected from Zon. Once we have that magnetism's formula, we can duplicate it here and then by the simple law of like charges repelling each other, we can deflect whatever magnetism they project at us."

"That's it exactly," the Amazon agreed. "What we have to do is find out the exact formula for their magnetism. There would seem to be only one way to do that. We—the Crusaders I mean—must go to Zon and see what we can discover."

Rijilon laughed shortly. "I'd warn you, Amazon, if you do that you'll never be heard of again and your Ultra will probably be destroyed."

The Amazon shrugged. "There are ways and means, my friend, and we have ample armory with which to protect ourselves... And the sooner we get on the move the better. Convey our compliments to the President and tell him what we are trying to do..." She got purposefully to her feet. "Ready, you others?"

They nodded—and within a short time were outside the building and at the spaceport. Once inside the Ultra it was only a matter of ten minutes before they were in the void, hurtling away towards the distant world of Zon.

"I don't want to question the rightness of what you're doing, Vi," Abna said, looking at her. "But what sort of plan have you in mind? Dealing with these Zonians won't be easy."

"It will if we come as friends," the Amazon answered, staring absently at the distant planet through the observation window.

"Friends? How do you mean?"

"Just this: we can go amongst them on the pretext that we wish to help them in their destructive plan against Karg. We can easily say we have been held prisoners on Karg and were sentenced to death, which is true. We can say we have just managed to escape, using Thania as a hostage to ensure that we got away safely."

Thania gazed in surprise as the Amazon's words were translated by the ever-operative Language Translator.

"I, a hostage?" she asked in surprise and the Amazon glanced at her.

"That will be your role in our plan of campaign, Thania. You must play the part of a girl who is our enemy, a girl whom we have supposedly stolen from Karg. You are supposed to have been the shield behind which we have escaped. You could have died on the spot if your own people had dared to stop us escaping. Understand?"

"Yes, but— It all sounds so strange."

"We do lots of strange things to achieve our ends," Abna told her, smiling. "As you'll discover after being with us for some time."

"Wouldn't it be quicker and more efficient to simply wipe out Zon and all it contains with the Zero Thought Amplifier?" Mexone asked bluntly. "Surely we're justified since the Zonians are planning to destroy Karg and the neighbor planets?"

"I don't doubt that we're justified," the Amazon replied, "but we'll only use the Amplifier as a last resort. We don't want to set ourselves up as the arbiters of life and death: we only want to stop wrong being done. We might even get the Zonians to see reason if we work hard enough and long enough."

"That I very much doubt," Viona commented. "However, there it is. We'll see what happens... Now come with me, Thania, and Mexone and I will give you a mental transfer of English with our mechanical educator during the trip."

Thania promptly obeyed. The Amazon, for her part, spent her time at the switchboard or else the window, until after a while Abna drifted over to her.

"Something's puzzling me," he murmured, and the Amazon glanced at him in surprise.

"Puzzling you? Forgive me, Abna, but I shouldn't have thought anything could."

"All right, I'll forgive the sarcasm. I know you don't really mean it. What puzzles me is your present kid glove attitude. Usually you're only too glad of a chance to be violent, and it's usually me who has to restrain you. This time everybody thinks it would be simpler to use the Zero Thought Amplifier and have done with it, yet you refuse to do it. Why? Your reason for withholding it didn't sound too convincing to me, especially when we're faced with cruel, merciless enemies."

"Don't you think it would be a good idea to discover if that is true before we destroy them?"

"True?"

"We have only the word of Rijilon, Railus, and the President, and we believed what we were told. I prefer to be sure for myself. We're friendly now with the people of Karg because it suited us to be so: If we can become as friendly with the Zonians we might find out the real circumstances. Then act as we see fit."

Abna spread his hands. "In fact discretion is the better part of valor, eh? All right. Vi. Have it your own way—but there's not the least doubt in my mind that the Zonians are all the men of Karg say they are..."

* * * *

In the course of time the formerly 'standstill' planet came within close proximity. Thania, Viona, and Mexone, having completed their transfer of the language, rejoined the Amazon and Abna to watch developments out of the window. Abna stood at the side of the Amazon as the Ultra moving at only a crawl, touched the outermost edge of the planet's atmosphere and thereafter began to descend towards what had appeared from their observations from space to be the principal city.

This, at least, was the Amazon's intention—but her eyes sharpened as, with Abna, she suddenly beheld at least a dozen spaceships sweeping up from the depths, evidently on a mission of inquiry.

"Committee of welcome," Abna commented dryly. Then he turned to Viona. "Connect the radio to the Language Translator, Viona. I have the feeling we're going to need it."

Viona obeyed, and by the time she had done so the oncoming spaceships had formed into a circle, ringing the Ultra completely and flashing a solitary light from their prows, which could only be interpreted as a stop signal.

The Amazon cut off the Ultra's power and waited for what should happen next. The great ship drifted aimlessly in the upper atmosphere, moved by the wind but slowly obeying the inevitable law of gravity, which was slowly dragging it downwards.

The radio buzzed for attention. Abna switched it on. A cold, unfriendly voice spoke.

"It is possible you do not understand our language—but if you do, understand this. You were given the order to stop your machine, not allow it to drift downwards towards the planet. If you understand my words, do as I have now ordered."

The Amazon smiled cynically and snapped a switch. The power plant came on again, distributing just enough power to keep the vessel from moving downwards. It floated in the wind currents… Then came the voice again.

"Evidently you understand my language. State your business here."

The Amazon said briefly: "We come as friends."

"Friends? From the world of Karg? That is difficult to believe."

"We came from Karg, but not because we are inhabitants of that planet. We are actually from a far distant galaxy and we landed on Karg expecting friendly cooperation. We did not get it. We escaped death by using a Kargian girl as a hostage, who is now with us. We wondered if friendship with you might be possible."

Long silence, then: "Your story would bear closer scrutiny, and so would this so-called hostage from Karg. I shall come aboard your vessel as a neutral observer, which means you will not attack me, nor shall I attack you. You understand?"

"I understand," the Amazon responded. "Draw alongside and anchor your airlock against ours. We will observe the neutral code as long as you do."

There followed the usual maneuvering, then presently the Zonian ship was in position. The Amazon moved the airlock switch and stood watching with the others as the swinging back of the immensely thick door revealed the view beyond—the view of the Zonian control room. There were six men in it, all of them in uniform and engaged in some duty obviously necessary to the control of the vessel… They had hard, unpleasant faces and pulled-down mouths. Their eyes were sharp and keen, an effect emphasized by the long peaks of the uniform-caps they wore.

Then presently one of them moved from the others and came through the tunnel created by the twin airlocks. He entered the Ultra's control room and looked about him—the quick, all-embracing look of a soldier and man of action. Silently the Crusaders studied him in their turn, noting the insignia and stars on the breast of his uniform and the military precision with which he moved and walked.

At length the Amazon made a move. She crossed to the radio equipment, restored the Language Translator to normal, and then looked at the Zonian as he watched her intently, possibly expecting an unfriendly move on her part.

"I am merely putting the Language Translator into action," she explained. "You may speak and be understood, even as you must now be able to understand me."

"I am Nio," he said curtly, laying a hand palm down on his broad chest in a curious kind of salute. "Commander Nio, in full control of this space fleet. I understood you to say you are from a distant galaxy, and that you happened—yes, happened was the word—to land on Karg. I do not find that explanation very convincing."

"It is none the less true," the Amazon said coldly, decided by now that she did not like Nio in the least degree. "I am known as the Golden Amazon of Earth, a planet so far distant you would not be able to comprehend the gulf. These other three"—she identified them—"are my colleagues, and here is the Kargian girl Thania, whom we are using as a hostage."

The piercing eyes looked from one to the other, then at length Nio seemed satisfied. He relaxed a trifle and began to pace slowly about the control room with an air of complete self-assurance.

"And you came to Zon to see if cooperation might be possible? Cooperation in what sense? You don't suppose you could teach us anything in the nature of science, do you? On the other hand, we certainly shan't hand any information to you, so what have either of us in common?"

"Even if we have no information to exchange, or science to give each other, there is sometimes something to be learned by friendly interchange of ideas. That is all we ask, if you will direct us to whoever is the controller of your planet."

Nio smiled cynically and stopped his pacing. He had come face to face with her and now stood surveying her, his feet apart and his hands on his hips, his whole attitude one of domineering arrogance.

"Apparently you expect quite a deal, Amazon! Understand now, and for always, that we are a race unto ourselves, and wish no cooperation or exchange of ideas with any other race—much less so with a woman who is probably very much in league with Karg, in spite of what you say to the contrary."

The Amazon said nothing, but there were danger lights glowing in her eyes.

"And the rest of you," Nio continued, swinging suddenly on his heel and surveying Abna, Viona, and Mexone each in turn. "You will naturally have the same story. Very well—let me tell you something!" Nio slapped his hand in vicious emphasis on the table. "Up till recently our world was paralyzed by a scientific trick which we were not quick enough to break. It is doubtful if the Kargians could think of a trick like that by themselves: it is far more likely that you—the so-called experts in science—helped the Kargians to paralyze us."

"On the contrary," the Amazon said. "We revived you. That thermodynamic prison of yours was unbreakable until we brought in a random element and released you. We would hardly do that if we were not friends, would we?"

Nio thought for a moment, then suddenly his right hand flashed out and gripped the arm of Thania. He whirled her to him fiercely.

"You—whatever your name is. You are a woman of Karg, are you not?"

"I—er—" Thania stared at his hard face in fright. "Yes, I am of Karg. My name is Thania."

"On one thing I am satisfied," Nio said, still holding her, "you are definitely one of the accursed ones of Karg. Your normal language is that of Karg: the language translation makes no difference to that basic fact. These others are not of Karg, to judge from their speech. So you, girl, can tell me much."

The Commander's iron grip on her arm slowly increasing. Thania shot a beseeching glance at the Amazon. For the moment, however, she made no move.

"Tell me…" Nio whispered. "Who are these people and what do they really want here?"

"Only to cooperate," Thania said.

"They plunged our world into apparent death, didn't they?"

"No. My own people did that… I have nothing in common with these four. I am their hostage, as they've already told you."

Nio pondered for a moment and then flung Thania away from him. She stumbled to a standstill beside the Amazon.

"You have great strength, Thania," the Amazon murmured. "Why don't you use it?"

"Because if I do I won't seen convincing. A girl of Karg would not have the steel muscles of a Crusader."

The Amazon looked vaguely surprised. This was something that had not occurred to her. If it did nothing else it showed the girl was endeavoring to cling to her role as hostage, no matter what.

"What," Nio demanded aggressively, "are you two women whispering about? I'll not have it! Understand?"

In the background Abna clenched his fists but he didn't act. He caught a brief glance from the Amazon, which, knowing her as he did, implied that she had not yet finished with the cocksure commander of the Zonian fleet.

"Why exactly you are here I do not seem able to discover," Nio said at length, "But I am prepared to think that it is for no good reason. Nothing worthwhile ever came from Karg—and you may as well know that since we recovered from our near-death a state of war has existed between Karg and ourselves."

"I was not aware of it," the Amazon said, and Nio gave a sneering smile.

"Not aware of it? I should have thought it would have been obvious, Amazon. If your world was paralyzed by another, and then you suddenly found release, what would you do? Naturally, the first thought would be reprisal for the wrong that had been done you."

Nobody spoke. Nio looked irritated, and then suddenly he whipped a gun from its holster and held it steadily. His eyes moved from one to the other.

"I don't intend to waste any more time. I demand to know your reason for being here."

"Otherwise you will shoot?" the Amazon asked quietly.

"Naturally."

"You came in here under a truce," Abna reminded him. "There is to be no violence on either side."

"Circumstances alter cases," Nio retorted. "I have no intention of being balked any longer."

The Amazon shrugged. "Well, since you put it that way you cannot expect us to observe neutrality if you don't." She glanced quickly at Abna. "Shut the airlock, Abna, and cut the others off."

He leapt to the switchboard, but before he could do anything Nio swung towards him. "Leave those switches alone, my friend! If you don't..."

Nio got no further. Viona, standing immediately beside him, lashed out her right hand and knocked the gun from his hand. He muttered something and dived for it, to fall his length as Mexone tripped him up. In those few moments other things happened too.

The men in the adjoining space machine leapt to their feet, intending to come to their commander's aid, but they had reckoned without Abna. He seized the foremost man as he came hurtling through the narrow tunnel, picked him up, and flung him into the midst of his fellows. Simultaneously, the Amazon closed the airlock switch, and cut off the magnetic grapples. There could only be one outcome to that—the leech-hold of the Zonian ship was broken, as also was the air current between it and the Ultra. It went reeling away into the gulf as the Ultra's airlock closed.

Evidently the outrush of air from their ship and its replacement by the zero void of space was too much for the Zonian soldiers for there was no sign of the ship's lock closing. It still went tumbling away into space, pulled towards the great disk of Zon itself hanging in the void.

"It appears your colleagues need no longer worry you—or us," the Amazon said, turning from the window to face Nio. "You have only yourself to blame. You should have respected your promise not to become hostile."

Nio did not say anything but his eyes flamed hatred. He was on his feet now, his fists clenched at his sides.

"You remarked that a state of war exists between Karg and your planet," the Amazon continued. "I am inclined to believe it now—and this is one particular facet of that war of which we are the masters."

"You overlook the rest of my fleet," Nio snapped. "You also overlook that you are in the midst of them."

"We'll deal with that if we have to," Abna said grimly; then he looked at the Amazon. "Well, Vi, what now? This fellow's no use to us, is he?"

"I'm not sure." The Amazon's smoldering eyes were fixed on him. "He obviously knows plenty: he may even know what we wish to discover. We can but see… Viona, cut off the radio. It's possible that Nio's soldiers may be overhearing what we're saying."

A switch snapped. Nio shifted uncomfortably, looking at the five ranged on all sides of him. Finally he gestured.

"Well, say something! What do you want to know? And don't

think I am the kind of weakling who'll reveal information just to save my own skin."

The Amazon said calmly: "You're no weakling, Nio; we give you credit for that much. As for saving your skin, that is not the usual practice in war, is it? However, you can tell us one thing: what kind of magnetism do you intend to use against Karg in order to steal its air and water?"

Nio's expression changed. "How do you know about that?"

"The Kargian Intelligence force discovered it long ago—the whole plan of the Zonians to steal air and water with which to clothe their artificial metal planet—"

"Then you *are* friendly with them! They would never have told you that, otherwise."

"So it is true then?" the Amazon asked. "Thanks for confirming it. You are a man of high standing in the Zonian order of things therefore you'll probably know what is intended and the kind of magnetism to be used—and when. I would suggest you tell us. It may be worth your life to do so."

Nio hesitated for a moment, then unexpectedly he flung himself forward, seized Thania—who was nearest to him—round the waist, and dragging her with him he backed to the radio set and switched it on. This done, he pulled the girl's gun from her belt and dug it in her back.

"Your Kargian hostage is proving quite useful," he commented. "Any attempt to stop me telling my fleet to destroy your ship will result in the girl dying instantly. I realize you don't want that to happen: she's too useful to you."

"Even assuming your fleet could destroy the Ultra, which is most unlikely," the Amazon said, "you'd be destroyed with it. Or did you think of that?"

"Certainly. My own life is useful only for the glory of Zon. If I die rather than betray a secret it matters but little."

"Rather than betray a secret?" Abna repeated. "Then you do know what we want to find out?"

Nio smiled and nodded coldly, hugging Thania tightly to him with one powerful arm. He turned to the radio and snapped on the microphone. Thania understood his words even if the others did not.

"Commander Nio speaking. Are you receiving me? Over."

"Receiving you, Commander. What are your orders? Over."

Thania, during his words, gave the Amazon a beseeching look. The Amazon nodded quietly—and in consequence nobody was more astounded than Nio when he abruptly found himself flying over the slim teenager's head, to crash with numbing force on the floor of the control room.

The radio loudspeaker chattered noisily, evidently demanding an answer from Nio—then it became quiet as the Amazon switched it off. She looked at Thania, slowly advancing towards the fallen Nio, and gave her a smile of encouragement.

CHAPTER 7

The blue haze

"What now?" Thania asked, as Nio got slowly to his feet and stared at her in amazement.

"Just deal with him," the Amazon responded, relaxing against the radio set. "You have good reason since you're the one he seems to have picked on all along. Perhaps you can even persuade him to give us the information we want. If not, Abna and I will have a try. At least we know he's got it: he just admitted the fact."

Thania nodded and straightened up. From the appearance of her she was nothing more than a slip of a girl in her black space tights, her fair hair tumbling rather crudely about her shoulders. Evidently Nio himself must have thought his temporary vanquishing was a fluke for he suddenly guffawed with laughter.

"At least you have a sense of humor, Amazon," he commented. "You must have to think that this—this child of Karg can do anything to make me talk. Even you couldn't do that—or Abna. But as for Thania here…"

Silence. Thania still gazed, her hands slack at her sides. Then Nio gave a shrug.

"This is nothing but a ridiculous interlude," he snapped, "and I have a radio order to give—"

He dived abruptly for the gun he had dropped, and Thania moved too with lightning speed. In a matter of seconds she had swept Nio's feet from under him with a scythe-like movement of her arms. Then even as he fell those same arms locked under his chin and the girl's knee was dug firmly in the small of his back.

"Very nice, Thania," the Amazon said, nodding her approval. "Now maybe we can make him talk."

She moved forward and looked down into Nio's strained face.

"It's up to you, Nio, to give us the information we want—namely: what kind of magnetism is going to be used against Karg. I'm afraid Thania may break your back or your neck if you don't speak. She's young and enthusiastic. Probably you're quite surprised to discover how strong she is? We're all as strong as she is, even stronger, so I'm afraid your much-vaunted toughness won't carry you very far."

The Amazon was smiling icily as she spoke and Nio was just commencing to realize the predicament he was in. Here were no ordinary people—as many others had discovered before him.

"Just speak," the Amazon suggested gently; then she gave a helpless lurch as something struck the Ultra from the outside with stupendous violence. She looked up quickly.

"A bomb of some kind," Abna said, peering through the window. "The fleet's mobilizing for attack."

"And they'll break you, and the ship," Nio whispered, unable to move for the iron pressure on his back and throat.

"Give them a taste of our weapons," the Amazon ordered. "But don't use the Zero-Thought Amplifier—at least not yet. Now, Thania, time's getting a bit short. How about coaxing our friend?"

The girl nodded and suddenly increased the backward pressure by two, three, and even four times, the muscles of her arms leaping up in rounded bunches beneath the elastic cloth of her tights... Nio gave a gasp, and then presently a hoarse cry. He tried by every means he could think of to dislodge the hold, but powerful man though he was he found it impossible—

Until another terrific concussion aided him. This was far worse than the earlier jolt—an atomic onslaught from outside that slewed the Ultra round giddily and brought a cracking sound from her outer plates. Instantly, Abna, Viona and Mexone were thrown from the control chairs of the weapons they were controlling, and the Amazon pitched helplessly into a corner. Thania, torn from her grip of Nio, went slithering along the floor and struck her head violently against the base of the switchboard.

The next thins she realized was that she was being jerked up by Nio, a gun prodding in her ribs.

"Over there," he snapped, waving his gun towards the wall. "You're too dangerous to—"

Nio never saw what happened next. With amazing speed, rivaling the Amazon herself at her best, Thania whipped up her right fist and planted it straight under Nio's jaw. Light exploded inside his head, blinding pain went through his neck, then his heavy body fell with a thud and remained motionless. Thania stared down at him in surprise, then looked at Abna questioningly as he struggled up and came to examine the fallen soldier.

"Congratulations, Thania," he said rather dryly. "You've broken his neck. "I'm afraid he won't tell us anything now."

"So the very thing we've wanted we've lost," the Amazon said regretfully. "Well, if we've done nothing else we've given you a workout, Thania. You're completely one of us now—"

She staggered again as once more the Ultra lurched, then her eyes glinted.

"I'll put up with this no longer," she snapped, and with a quick stride went over to the protonic gun and settled herself in the saddle. Then while she focused the sights she added, "Get rid of Nio's body through the trap, Abna— Ah, so that's the baby that's causing the trouble!"

Her eyes narrowed as she looked through, the sights. Of the eleven or so machines flying around the Ultra one in particular was bristling with all manner of different-colored beams, whilst bombs themselves were visibly being released as tiny, gleaming points of light that came straight for the Ultra.

The Amazon pressed the protonic gun's button. Instantly a rain of protons slammed into the midst of the annoying vessel and it exploded outwards from the center in a mass of boiling metal and intolerable flame. A direct hit, which evidently had also exploded whatever bombs it had on board. At that violent disintegration, the rest of the vessels changed course and then began to streak downwards towards their home planet. Viona and Mexone grinned as they watched them go.

"That seems to have scared them off," Viona commented. "Maybe they'll realize next time that tackling the Ultra isn't so easy as it looks."

Abna came into the control room from the main passage and glanced across at the Amazon.

"Nio disposed off," he announced. "I used the ejector-trap. At the moment his body's hurtling down in the wake of those space machines. Apparently we've won the first round."

"And lost it," the Amazon sighed. "We haven't got the secret of the magnetism we wanted, and we certainly can't descend to Zon and pose as friends after what's happened—so it looks as though the only thing to do is to return to Karg and tell them we've failed in our mission."

Abna nodded gloomily. "Which isn't a pleasant thing to have to do."

The Amazon slid from the proton gun stool and came over to the switchboard. Thania caught at her arm as she did so.

"Amazon, I didn't do wrong, did I? I simply hit at Nio when I saw he'd got the gun. I never intended to break his neck."

"Just one of those things," the Amazon shrugged. "We'll find some other way of getting at what we want."

With that she turned to the switches, and set the Ultra turning slowly until her nose was pointed at distant Karg. Then speed began to build on speed as the forty-million mile hop was made.

"The sooner we get back the better," the Amazon said. "There may be a way of evacuating the Kargians from their planet before disaster comes. There's little doubt now that Karg will be the first to suffer even if that wasn't the original intention... In the meantime we'd better get ourselves cleaned up a bit after the rough-house we've had."

* * * *

Two hours later, when the Ultra was more than half way back towards Karg, something happened—and it caught the five in the control room by surprise. There was a vast jerk from the Ultra, a groaning from the atomic power plant, and then a noticeable slowing down. Instantly the Amazon was at the switchboard checking the instruments, with Abna immediately behind her.

"Funny," the Amazon muttered, frowning. "We've lost five thousand miles an hour of our speed, and it's still dropping. Look!"

Abna nodded tensely, his eyes on the main velocimeter. The red needle that dominated it was swinging slowly backwards on its graded scale. He studied it for a moment, then hurried over to the power plant. It was still functioning perfectly, but his attuned ear detected a shrill wheezing note, a sure sign that it was straining against something—an unheard of circumstance in free outer space.

"There's a sort of blue haze out here," Viona said, surveying through the observation window. "And I can't see any sign of a planet or dead star which might be exerting its influence... Just a blue haze. It can't be a star anyway," she added suddenly. "We'd have noticed it on our way out."

"What's that?" Thania demanded, pointing down towards her own planet. "In the haze—a sort of bulge on the side of Karg—"

"Bulge?" Viona stared at it and then gave a start. "Good heavens! What is it?"

The Amazon and Abna hurried to her side and watched the phenomenon for a moment. Something was definitely swelling like a small pear from the limb of the distant world, stretching outwards into infinity and surprisingly enough coming straight towards the Ultra.

"I've got it!" Abna exclaimed abruptly, snapping his fingers. "It's frozen air and water being dragged from Karg—magnetic power which shows as a blue haze is stripping the planet as one might peel a banana. The magnetic drag is slowing us up."

"You mean the Zonians have acted already?" Thania exclaimed in horror

"Doesn't seem to be much doubt of it, does there? We know that they had everything ready even before paralysis overtook them. They have had time by now to adjust themselves— Anyway, there's no doubt about that." And Abna nodded to the growing gray-white ball hurtling through the void.

Suddenly the Amazon leapt to the switchboard and increased power to maximum. The Ultra ceased its slowed-down progress for a moment and noticeably leapt forward, but still the enormous magnetism from Zon was having its effect for the great vessel did not maintain progress. It began to very gradually slow down once more.

"We'd better turn aside—if we can," the Amazon said, with a quick glance. "For one thing we don't want to be dragged to Zon, and for another we want to get out of the way of that frozen ice and air when it arrives. It may prove dangerous, and our outer plates have already taken a good deal of punishment from those bombs used by the fleet—"

She began to operate the controls swiftly, then paused as Abna caught at her arm.

"Wait a moment, Vi: there's something we might as well do first. We're right in the midst of the magnetic stream so we can take a reading of it—find out its frequency, power, and all about it. We missed getting it from Nio, but we needn't miss this."

He turned aside and began working swiftly on the detectors, writing down notes as he progressed. The Amazon waited, her anxious eyes on the frozen air and water growing ever larger in the gulf of space.

"Do you think it's any use knowing the formula now?" she asked. "Zon's stripped Karg completely from the look of things, so we're too late to save it."

"Maybe, but there are other planets to be considered. We might as well have the formula as not..." Abna scribbled busily, then at last he nodded. "Right! I'll work it out properly later. I've got all the details. Start swinging us aside."

"Easier said than done," the Amazon muttered, resuming her activity with the controls.

Just how difficult a task it was became apparent in a few moments as, exerting every vestige of atomic power in the plant, the Amazon struggled to force the Ultra off-course—and out of the magnetic influence, and incidentally out of the way of the onrushing frozen air and water. But the plant, mighty though it was, was not up to it. It groaned under the terrific strain and time and again fuses blew— to be hastily repaired by Abna, Viona, or Mexone as they stood by. Thania, for her part, stood by the window and reported the progress of the stolen oceans and atmosphere from her planet. The mass had come close enough now to blot out the view of distant Karg itself.

"We can't do it," the Amazon said finally, relaxing slightly. "We haven't enough power. In a few moments we'll stop altogether and then begin to move backwards towards Zon—"

"No we won't," Abna retorted. There's one chance yet, and one we've never needed to take—but we will now. We'll triple the power of the plant." And he darted to the passageway that led to the great storage holds.

"Triple the power of the plant?" Viona repeated in amazement. "What on earth does he mean by that? The plant won't stand it: it'll blow the fuses every time."

"Probably so," the Amazon agreed, "but in the brief overrun

we'll get we may manage to pull out— It'll necessitate repairs once we're out of the magnetism."

Abna came back in a hurry, two large copper cubes in his arms. He nodded quickly to the Amazon and she switched off the power long enough for him to place the cubes in the power plant's matrix. In these few moments the Ultra slowed down alarmingly.

"Okay," Abna said curtly. "Switch on—full power."

The Amazon obeyed, and this time the power plant screamed as it overran itself, Fuses blew instantly and were instantly replaced. Precious seconds were gained whilst the fuses held out, seconds in which the Ultra's ponderous mass swung off course and actually accelerated slightly against the magnetic drag...

So it went on—seconds gained and fuses blown. Replacement of fuses, and on again. But little by little the Ultra was moving diagonally as well as forward, tearing herself out of the vastly powerful magnetic stream being projected from Zon—

It seemed a matter of hours to the straining, sweating five in the control room, but actually it was only a matter of ten minutes at the most, and at the end of that ten minutes the Ultra suddenly gave an enormous spurt, so violent indeed that all five fell backwards and to the floor, pinned there by a violent and instantaneous acceleration.

What had happened was plain enough to the Amazon—and to the others too, probably. The Ultra had finally pulled out of the stream of magnetism with an acceleration equivalent to three times the full power of the atomic plant. Suddenly meeting no resistance whatever, no friction, no anything at all, she achieved within second the maximum power of the tripled plant and was almost instantly moving through space, traveling faster and faster.

It was only the degravitators and stabilizers built into the vessel that saved the five, otherwise moving at that unthinkable velocity they would have been crushed into and merged with the very metal floor onto which they had been flung. Even as it was, one by one the Crusaders lapsed into unconsciousness.

The ship hurtled on through space, its speed increasing to an appreciable percentage of the speed of light itself, the maximum possible velocity in normal space.

It was the Amazon who regained consciousness first—only to find that the acceleration was still continuing. She began to move slowly, every slightest movement taking her ages to accomplish—

and even then she could not have done it but for her superhuman strength. With her face a taut mask of strain and mighty effort she struggled first on to one knee, then after an interminable pause struggled to the other.

Again a long interval—then with muscles rolling under her black tights she fought her way to her feet and reached out to the switchboard, supporting her right arm by placing her left hand under her elbow. Even so, the limb felt as heavy as a building and her legs were near to cracking with the weight of her torso.

Perspiration streaming down her face she gripped the power lever and pulled down and out…

Instantly the crushing weight vanished as acceleration ceased. The ship was still moving at incredible velocity, but with the force of acceleration removed there was no longer its drag to contend with. The stabilizers acted as they had always done, set at Earth-norm attraction.

The Amazon slumped to the floor, breathing hard. Within a few minutes of the crushing pressure being lifted the others had recovered and were commencing to look about them.

"Whew!" the Amazon muttered, drawing the back of her hand over her streaming face. "We wanted to move and we certainly did!"

The others nodded rather ruefully and got slowly to their feet. Thania in particular was awe-struck: this unexpected demonstration of velocity at almost the speed of light was something entirely new. She crossed to the Amazon's side with wonder in her gray eyes.

"What an amazing vessel this is," she murmured. "There's no other machine in the universe which can keep up with it, surely?"

"Not many, anyway," the Amazon replied. "We've encountered a few in our experiences… However, that's beside the point. The thing is that we've lost your system of worlds completely for the moment."

"We've traveled so far and so fast, you mean?"

"Exactly." As Abna cut off the power plant and restored it to normal, the Amazon looked out of the window. The Ultra was still moving with unbelievable speed, and only slightly began to slow down as Abna switched on the power again in reverse.

"We'll be a long time getting ourselves straight," Abna announced finally. "It will take some considerable time to slow up traveling as we are at about 90 percent of the speed of light. Once we've done that we'll try and find our way back to Karg. And I say 'try' advisedly, because we're billions of miles away from away from Thania's system."

* * * *

It was many hours later before the Ultra finally became manageable again, and at the end of this time she had slowed down sufficiently to be swung round to face the direction of travel—then began the reverse process to recover the distance lost. Of necessity, however, the Amazon was only able to build up speed gradually, to prevent a repeat of the previous crushing acceleration on the outward journey.

"It shouldn't be too difficult to find our way back to Karg eventually," the Amazon said, after studying the instruments. "In space, unless drawn aside by a gravitation of some kind, everything moves in a straight line—which includes the Ultra. Therefore, since we haven't turned aside in the slightest degree, we'll simply follow the same course in reverse and that should bring us back to within the vicinity of Karg. It will have moved in its orbit—and the system of which it is part will also have moved because of galactic drift, but it should still be within visual range. We shall take a long time over it because of course we're not going to move at even a tenth of the outward velocity—so we might as well make ourselves as comfortable as possible during the journey. And we'll have a meal whilst we're about it."

So the backward journey commenced—a thing of tedium to the Amazon, Abna, Viona, and Mexone, accustomed as they were to enormous journeys through the wastes of space—but a thing of wonder to Thania, lost for hours at a time in contemplation of the hosts of heaven.

Altogether, it occupied two weeks—reckoned from the time of their initial departure—to arrive back at the point where Karg, Zon, and the other planets and parent sun were visible and recognizable. Only then did the Amazon take the Ultra in hand and steer it on a fixed course towards distant Karg. Remotely, beyond it, lay Zon—since the Ultra was approaching from the opposite side of the system on this occasion—and more remotely still beyond Zon itself yet another world—a planet of grayish hue visible only as a dot illuminated by the distant sun.

"That will be the metal world which the Zonians have created," the Amazon murmured, as Abna studied space with her. "And from the look of things they've already started to give it an atmosphere."

"Yes—Karg's atmosphere," Abna agreed grimly. "And oceans underneath presumably. And it will go on until the other planets have been robbed too, to provide the correct density of air and water... Incidentally, what does Karg look like now?"

The Amazon turned to the telescope and focused it. For a long tine she studied slowly approaching Karg in silence, then with a grim face she looked up.

"Look for yourself, Abna," she invited. "What I think about it is best left unsaid."

Not only Abna but each one in the party looked in turn, and to them, there was revealed a vision of chaos and ruin. In the first place the planet was cloudless due to its stripped atmosphere, and what air there was left—if any—was so slight that it rendered the surface of Karg crystal-clear. But it was no longer a world of thriving cities and immense industry, of quiet progress and genial cooperation. It looked like a gigantic battlefield, every vestige of its surface cratered and pitted, with a vast patchwork of broken hills of metal and stone. Karg had been scourged to the uttermost and it was doubtful if anything lived on its surface anymore.

Thania was the last to look. She could not help her eyes filling with tears as she looked at the Amazon.

"My world—seems to be messed up badly," she said, biting her lip. "In fact it's a ruin. I would never have thought I could feel like this about a planet, particularly with my parents dead. But it was my birthplace, and I had friends there..." her voice broke, and she looked away for a moment.

"I understand, Thania—perfectly," the Amazon said, patting her shoulder gently. Then her expression changed a little. "Don't worry, the Zonians are going to pay for this—to the uttermost limit. I promise you that."

"And you still don't intend using the Zero Thought Amplifier?" Abna asked. "You don't surely think there's any doubt now that the Zonians are a terrible menace?"

"I still hesitate at mass elimination," the Amazon responded. "I think we'll have a look at Karg, assess the damage, and then decide."

Abna shrugged. "In which case they might attack the remaining planets, Vi. I'm not usually an advocate for destruction, but in this case we have every justification. We've seen what these devils are up to and the damage they've caused."

The Amazon hesitated, then she caught another glimpse of Thania's troubled face. That decided her.

"All right," she said, nodding. "We'll us our ultimate weapon and put an end to this kind of thing."

"Good," Abna said quietly. "On this occasion I can't see that there's anything wrong in it. Anything wrong or hurtful to others ought to be wiped out. That's only commonsense—"

The Amazon turned to the switchboard and moved the switches. The Ultra changed its steady course towards Karg and swung round until it directly faced Zon. Then it began to advance swiftly, the computers calculating for the planet's orbital movement. Thania watched the maneuvers and then came to the Amazon's side.

"Amazon, what is the Zero Thought Amplifier? I've heard you mention it before. Why is it so terrible?"

The Amazon smiled gravely. "It's terrible, Thania, because it cancels out anything material instantly. Actually, it is a mathematical machine of the highest degree of efficiency and was given to us as a gift on a distant world for some service or other that we performed. There it is, by the window."

Thania gazed at it—a box-like affair of shiny black with a lens on the front and switches at the side, the whole being mounted on the swivel-head of a tripod.

"It doesn't look particularly startling," she said.

"Appearances are deceptive, Thania. It has self-contained atomic batteries and a million miles of range. Thought is concentrated into it—one thought only, namely the thought of the zero-quantity of a cipher. That, mathematically expressed, means the substance of nothing, if I may call it that."

"It sounds a bit crazy."

"That I grant you, but consider the thought of zero amplified an infinite number of times and projected as a solid beam of concentration on any object. Inevitably the object disappears because thought is a higher state than materiality. The thought—vastly amplified—of nothing wipes out a material object without trace... Now perhaps you can see why it is such a dangerous weapon."

"Yes, I do. Indeed I do..."

"Before long, you'll see it in action," the Amazon promised. "Then you'll perhaps consider that Karg has been avenged."

With that the Amazon relapsed into silence, and in the main said little as she guided the Ultra steadily through the void, on the lookout all the time for possible interference from Zon. None came, however, and at last the instruments showed that the Ultra was within range of the planet. She took the Ultra into a low orbit, and gave Abna a significant glance.

"Ready?" Abna asked, turning to the Zero Amplifier and adjusting the controls.

"It's up to you," she said. "If you find your single-handed concentration isn't sufficient to wipe out an entire planet we'll augment your efforts. Have a try, anyway."

Abna sighted the instrument on the planet and then adjusted the power pointer to maximum. The Amazon watched him and then glanced at Thania.

"The concentrated radiations pass through the window glass without harm," she explained. "Chiefly because the glass is so made that it has invisible interstices in it through which the radiations pass. A touch of a switch opens the interstices by polarizing the atoms, and any loss of air there might be within the control room here is hardly noticeable, and soon made up afterwards, anyhow."

Abna depressed the switch on the wall, which operated the window glass and then glanced at the others.

"Ready—if you want to come and look," he said, and immediately the Amazon, Viona, Mexone, and Thania gathered before the outlook window and gazed down on the teeming planet that had brought such destruction to Karg.

A switch snapped, then Abna threw every scrap of his concentration into the machine, looking at the same time into the faint coppery beam it was emanating as it fanned outwards, to finally encompass all of Zon when at the limit of its extent... The seconds passed, the power hummed steadily, but there was not the least sign of anything happening. Thania shot a puzzled look at the Amazon and she herself glanced at Abna.

"What's gone wrong, Abna?"

He shook his head worriedly. "I wish I knew!"

Ceasing his concentrations he examined the apparatus carefully, but as far as he could tell all was well. The Amazon lent her aid, but she too was as mystified as he was.

"We'll try a test target," she said finally. "If you can destroy that but not Zon I think I know what the answer is."

Crossing to the switchboard, she ejected a flying ball of metal from the Ultra. It went sailing outwards into space and in a matter of seconds Abna had it focused in the path of the Amplifier beam. Again he concentrated on the zero quantity and instantly the metal ball vanished into nothing. Thania blinked with the suddenness of it.

"It worked that time," she remarked, glancing. "Perhaps a whole planet is too big to attempt?"

"A planet or a speck of dirt—it makes no difference as long as the width of the beam encompasses it," Abna said. "Only answer I can think of here is that the matter of Zon doesn't somehow respond."

"I thought of that, too," the Amazon remarked. "We've come across that sort of thing before—but on that occasion the matter we wanted to destroy was immune because it wasn't even of this Universe, This definitely is—so the only answer is that Zon must be shielded by a transparent shell of repulsive force of some kind from which the amplified radiations bounce off."

"Even then…" Abna stood thinking. "Wouldn't one call a shell of repulsive force matter? Matter in its basic force state?"

"Perhaps so—but not matter in the sense that we understand it—like a solid world. Too tenuous to be resolved, I'm afraid. Come to think of it, it's only natural that the Zonians will protect their planet between the air-and-water thefts—and that seems to be what we're up against."

"Which means," Abna said slowly, switching off the Amplifier, "that we have to wait until they remove the repulsive screen. That will only come when spaceships want to come out into the void, or when they decide to attack another planet with their magnetism… Maybe days or weeks," he finished gloomily.

The Amazon crossed to the switchboard. "We'll have to wait for a more favorable opportunity, that's all. Best thing we can do at the moment is return to Karg, as we intended at first, and assess the damage."

Her mind made up she switched on the power plant, turned the Ultra around, and began the trifling forty million mile hop across the void to Karg once more. As she watched the instruments her thoughts were busy—and they were none too happy thoughts, either. The failure of the Amplifier, the ultimate weapon she had fully intended using if everything else had failed was now proved as useless: and if an attempt were made to eliminate the planet when the shell was removed it would also mean braving that magnetism, which as events had shown could not be done. On the face of it the Zonians were winning in all directions, and for the life of her the Amazon could not think of any sound method by which to defeat the brilliant scientists who were determined to clothe their own specially created world at the expense of their neighbors.

"Any ideas?" Abna asked quietly, and the Amazon started. She had not realized he had been watching her.

"For once—none," she confessed.

"We'll tackle them when they remove their screen. Rely on it."

The Amazon sighed. "I wish we could—but they'll only remove it to project their magnetism, and we dare not get involved in that. That's what I was just thinking about. One state's as bad as the other. We'll have to think of something that will break that shell of energy of theirs—and that won't be easy."

Abna nodded and fell to thought. He had not arrived at any worthwhile conclusion by the time Karg had been reached, however, so for the time being he gave up thinking about the matter and concentrated on more immediate things. He stood watching as the Ultra swept down from the upper levels and flew over what had once been a great metropolis. Now it was nothing more than a tangled heap of rubble and dust. There were however one or two landmarks that by a fluke had been left standing, and from these the Amazon took her bearings, landing finally on what she judged was the remains of the air and sky port.

She cut off the power plant and then stood looking outside in the heavy silence that had dropped.

CHAPTER 8

Second attack

Abna was the first to speak. "We'd better not risk going outside in the ordinary way. I'll see what air there is first."

He crossed to the instruments, which connected with the exterior and read them. Then a low whistle escaped him.

"Air pressure's cut down to a tenth of what it was," he said. "Humidity and water vapor register almost zero. Temperature around ninety Fahrenheit due to the thinness of the air. With our kind of physique we ought to be able to just about manage… Anyway, here goes."

He pulled the airlock switch and slowly the immense door opened. Within the control room there was a faint hissing as the air escaped into the lesser density outside, then for each Crusader, as they stepped out into the hot exterior, there was a sense of tremendous constriction about the chest—a feeling as though an iron hoop were girding them. So thin was the air they were quite unable to take a deep breath, and the slightest exertion made even their immensely strong hearts pound uncomfortably.

"They certainly managed to strip this planet effectively," Abna said grimly, as they walked along slowly amidst the rubble and looked about them. "It looks as though a nuclear bomb has hit the place. Hardly one stone standing on another."

The Amazon did not answer. She had come to a sudden halt and was peering under her hand at something in the distance. The blaze of the sun made it difficult to see properly. The haze of dust in the air somehow diffused the light and made distant scenes uncertain. Yet she was convinced there was something on the move a couple of miles away— After a moment or two she was satisfied that her belief was correct. A straggling party of men and women was approaching. Before long they became revealed as a scared, hungry-looking party in dusty and bedraggled clothes. They said something as they came up, but of course it was quite unintelligible. The Amazon glanced at Thania.

"You understand the language, Thania. What do they say?"

"They say that they saw the Ultra land and were under the impression that we are enemies. They've come to give themselves up."

The Amazon nodded. "Tell them that we're friends and only anxious to help. Ask them if there are any more survivors. Get to know all the details. In particular try and find out if Rijilon or Railus are still alive."

The girl turned back to the group and a long exchange of information began. Finally she seemed satisfied with what she had learned and turned back to the Amazon.

"There seem to be quite a few survivors and most of them are in a roughly constructed town two miles to the north. From what I can gather, Railus has survived but the President and Rijilon have disappeared. If we go to the town we might be able to learn more."

"All right, let's go," the Amazon said, and led the tramp across the dusty stones and debris with the dejected-looking survivors trailing in the background.

Throughout the entire journey there were still the evidences of total or partial destruction. The one thing absent seemed to be fires— usually one of the most dominating features of a grand catastrophe. Then the Amazon remembered that several weeks had been lost by herself and the others in space, and in that time any fires had obviously been extinguished or else burned themselves out in the thin air.

So finally the party came to a region where a rough town had been constructed—a town composed mainly of crude huts which in themselves were created out of the more serviceable debris. There were numerous fires burning around which families were doing their best to cook meals. Warmth, fortunately, was not a hazard in the blazing sunlight.

To arrive in the 'town' was only part of the problem, however, as far as the Crusaders were concerned. They spent endless time wandering amongst the people—Thania doing all she could to learn facts from them—until at last they managed to trace Railus himself to a shoddy habitation of metal sheeting and timber. He was actually inside the shack when the five arrived and peered in the narrow entrance way.

Railus's look of astonishment was complete when he saw them. There was no doubt that it was him, with his massive forehead and spare figure. The only thing different about him was the beard he had grown and the shabbiness of his clothes.

Instantly he burst forth into welcoming greetings and helped the party inside. He motioned to rough sackings and torn cushions as the only alternative to chairs—then he sat back and looked at them questioningly.

"He's more than glad to see us," Thania interpreted. "He thought we had gone for good. I've explained to him how we got unexpectedly shot into space and then had to find our way back."

"Ask him what happened here," the Amazon directed.

There was a long exchange of language; then Thania turned.

"He says the air and oceans were stripped away in a huge cataclysm which destroyed everything on the planet. Tens of thousands of people, as well as buildings, sea, and air, were drawn away to distant Zon and there are only a few hundred people left on the planet. If no further attack is made they'll survive, and a scientific method will be found to restore the air to normal and replace the lost oceans... But that is the work of years."

The Amazon said: "Repeat this to him. We have done everything in our power to wipe out Zon—using our most devastating weapons, but we've failed completely. We have, however, got to the formula of the magnetism the Zonians use—which was the thing we set out to get. It is unlikely that this world will be attacked again for there is hardly enough air and water left for it to be worth the Zonians' while to extract it—and they certainly won't waste their power on trying to blot out the survivors. They're after bigger things than that— namely, the stripping of the three neighbor worlds, which so far are untouched. We can save one of them if we can get in touch with their scientists. Tell him that."

Thania did so. Then: "He says why can you only save one world out of three?"

"Because," the Amazon answered, "we don't know which planet

the Zonians will attack next. If it should happen to be the world we protect then we might manage to save more than one. It's a matter of chance."

Thania interpreted and then asked a question: "Railus asks what you propose to do."

"He knows the plan we discussed. Since we know what magnetism the attackers will use we can arrange to have a like charge thrown back at them, which will repel their magnetism and upset their arrangements. Which of the neighbor scientists is the best able to build the defense we require?"

There was a moment or two before Thania translated back. "It would appear that the world nearest to us—Biuz by name—would be the best. The scientists are of a high caliber, and also the civilization is of a friendly order. Railus doesn't doubt but what cooperation would be simple to obtain, particularly when it is realized how extreme the danger is. He will come with us to assist."

The Amazon said: "Speed is our main worry. How soon can we leave?"

"Immediately," Thania replied in a moment. "Railus agrees with you that there is not a minute to be lost…"

* * * *

Within thirty minutes the Ultra was on its way once more, the world of Karg falling into space behind. Railus, for his part, shaved, washed, and changed into attire loaned him by the Crusaders, then after a meal he went into conference with Abna over the notes he had made of the Zonian magnetism.

Long before the journey to Biuz was completed, the Ultra's computers had worked out Abna's figures to the last decimal, providing an exact formula from the original readings he had made. As he studied the results carefully—the figures having been translated for him by Thania—Railus nodded his domed head in satisfaction.

."There shouldn't be anything difficult about this, my friends," he said finally, and the Language Translator promptly transcribed his words. "As I mentioned through Thania, the Biuzian scientists are quite accomplished. The only thing that worries me is: shall we have the time? It will not be the work of a moment to build this repulsive system. It will take several weeks."

"That we'll have to gamble on," the Amazon said. "There's also the chance that another planet might be attacked first, and if so that gives us more time—and, unfortunately, destroys another planet before we can aid it. The situation is full of hazards like that but I think we may erect whatever we need before disaster overtakes us, to say nothing of the Biuzians. The scientists of Zon will no doubt require a little while to gather their power again for the supreme effort."

Railus nodded slowly and gazed through the window. His finely intellectual face took on an unusual hardness.

"All this destruction, this suffering, to satisfy the insane greed of a race who put science before soul," he muttered. "Look at that distant gray world out there, clothed now with the air and water which have been stolen from our planet... The Zonians have done their job magnificently—part of it at least—if only they had not had to resort to such inhumanity in order to accomplish it."

"And if only I hadn't wandered on Zon's surface and caused it all to become possible," Thania sighed. "That is one of the mistakes of my life, which I shall never forget."

"All of us make mistakes," Viona said quietly. "No use to keep talking about it, Thania. You can't blame yourself for a moment."

But it was plain the girl did, even though she said no more... Then Railus turned from the window and asked a question.

"How long before we reach Biuz, my friends?"

Abna glanced at the switchboard. "Say another hour."

"Good! The sooner the better... And I cannot thank you enough, my friends, for the wonderful effort you are making on our behalf—at considerable danger to yourselves, too."

"It's one of our tasks in life to help," Abna smiled.

"And considering it is self-imposed it is a very noble one. I am only too sorry there was so much misunderstanding at the outset—However, that is over and done with, like the civilization which was responsible for it." Railus's face clouded for a moment with unhappy recollections, then he shrugged the mood off. "If only we can succeed in this venture, Amazon, and hold the Zonians in check, there can be peace in our system for ages to come."

"Can there ever be that with Zon in the system?" Mexone asked pointedly. "Even if they get balked this time they will still be there, a perpetual threat—always a jump ahead of you in knowledge. I don't think there'll ever be real peace for you until they are utterly eliminated."

Railus nodded moodily—and for some reason Mexone's words seemed to impress Thania. She gave him a quick look, her gray eyes full of the brightness of a sudden thought—then she relaxed again and returned to gazing out of the window...

So the journey to Biuz was finally completed—a distance of 68 million miles. From above Biuz looked much the same as Karg had done before the catastrophe—and at ground level the effect was confirmed. Biuz was a thriving planet, crowded with beings exactly like the Kargians in physique, and following more or loss the same industrial inclinations.

Within half an hour of landing in the main metropolis, Railus's high scientific station and reputation within the system was sufficient for him to gain an audience for himself and the Crusaders with the presiding ruler of Biuz—for in the manner as Karg, Biuz was not split into different states and ideologies, but had one supreme controller and a panel of experts to help him, elected by the people.

He was tall and grave, with a rather sunken but highly intelligent face. With a portable language translator to help out, he listened with impassive gravity to the story Railus and the Crusaders had to tell, and his response to them was immediate.

"We are not altogether in ignorance of what has happened," he said finally. "We knew from telescopic observation that something of a diabolically destructive nature had struck your world, Railus—but following our policy never to interfere in a neighbor world's internal affairs, we made no special investigation. We suspected an explosion had occurred—but the truth you bring to us is disquieting. Disquieting indeed..."

Long silence. Then the Amazon said, "Nothing less, Controller, than the destruction of your world too, sooner or later, unless you accede to the plan we've worked out. That way the Zonians can be forestalled—and later we may find a way to crush them forever."

"The Zonians," the Controller mused. "The Accursed Ones they are called in our history records. Always stirring up trouble and strife. I really thought the situation was under control when you, Railus, and your fellow scientists devised the system of thermodynamic equilibrium."

Railus shrugged. "Something went wrong, Controller, and Zon

revived, with disastrous consequences as far as our planet was concerned. However, to more immediate matters. Am I correct in assuming that you agree to this counter-magnetism system?"

"Undoubtedly." The Controller rose with sudden decision. "I will make arrangements for our scientists to have immediate translated copies of this formula of yours, and our industries and labor will be marshaled for the construction of the necessary towers and power-houses throughout the planet. Let us hope we will be in time to save ourselves. You, I take it, will stay here and supervise?"

Railus reflected for a moment, then: "When you have labor and engineering geared up for action we'll certainly supervise, but for the moment I think we can occupy ourselves more usefully by visiting the other planets in the system and warning them, as we have you. At least they may have a chance of to save themselves."

"As you wish," the Controller smiled. "I will expect you back as soon as..." His voice slowed down and finally stopped. He stood mute, his head cocked a little on one side, listening.

"Strange," he murmured, "that there should be a wind rising. You hear it? In this mechanically-controlled climate of ours I should have thought—"

Suddenly there was chaos! The gently moaning wind which all could hear rose in a matter of second to a screaming roar, then with an explosion like a bomb the entire room in which the six stood crashed inwards, the massive walls bowing and breaking before an irresistible force.

The Controller stumbled and fell, to almost instantly vanish under a smother of debris. Somehow together, though hardly able to stand on their feet, the Crusaders stared incredulously at stone and steel hurtling skywards in a colossal vortex. With the spinning, screaming debris went the Controller, the furniture, the walls, valuable instruments, papers—the lot, flashing skywards as a terrific power drew them. In a second Railus was gone too, struggling helplessly.

"The—the Zonians again!" the Amazon panted, as she and the others held onto each other in the face of hurricane wind. "Got to— get to the Ultra somehow!"

Hardly realizing what they were doing, the breath knocked down their throats, they stumbled and reeled out of the collapsing building. Outside in what had been the street there was an amazing vision as traffic, peoples, and smaller buildings shot to the writhing sky.

Nothing could withstand the pulling force aimed at Biuz, and as the Crusaders well knew it was the finish for them too if the magnetic power happened to settle dead upon them.

Lashed by the hurricane wind, their ears filled with the roaring thunder of a tunnel torn through the planet's atmosphere, they lurched and floundered along the shattered main street towards the spot where they had left the Ultra—if it still happened to be there! It was a journey through hell. Time and again they were flattened to the ground by the wind. Time and again they caught at each other or the foundations of a building to save themselves being whisked skywards—and inch by inch they progressed, their faces and bodies lashed with flying stones and the shrapnel of metallic pieces.

Their journey seemed to take hours as all around them the city was disintegrated and whirled upwards, to the accompaniment of almost unimaginable noise. Glancing upwards once the Amazon had the amazing vision of men and women flying helplessly aloft as the roaring wind or the actual magnetism caught them—then abruptly she was hanging on to Thania with all her power as the girl was dragged from the roadway as though there were an invisible cord about her.

The Amazon needed all her strength to win the battle to save the girl, but with Abna's help she succeeded and flung Thania flat on her face.

"We'd better all do that!" Abna shouted into the wind. "If we get down into one of these holes we'll perhaps be safer."

The hole he referred to was actually a sewer entrance with the manhole cover torn off. Still struggling with wind and magnetism the five crawled into it and little by little descended the metal steps down into the well's wall—until finally they felt water beneath them. They continued the descent and finished up with water flowing round their knees and rushing into dark distances. The mephitic odor of sewer gas set them coughing, but at least it was better than the possibility of being whisked into outer space at any moment.

"Obviously we're too late to save this planet," Abna commented bitterly, at length.

"Obviously," the Amazon agreed. "I shouldn't be at all surprised if Zonian telescopes haven't been trained on us, and when it was seen we took the Ultra to Biuz they unleashed their magnetism. They couldn't have known that we came to try and erect a defense system—so the only assumption is that they hope to wipe us out."

"Which means they're afraid of us," Viona said. "I wonder if we ought to feel complimented?"

There was silence for a moment. Roaring chaos about and the gurgle and splash of evil-smelling waters below. Then came the Amazon's voice.

"If the Ultra's survived this and hasn't been dragged away with the rest of things, we'll have to move to the next planet as fast as possible and warn them. This time we may have the opportunity to be in time. The Zonians will be bound to take a certain interval to get themselves ready for their next attack, besides having to transfer the present lot of stolen air and water to their metal planet. Unfortunately, they've had all the time we were away in deep space. If we move at top speed we may be quick enough to defeat them."

"It'll take us all our time," Viona said soberly. "Don't forget we've got to establish contact before we can even turn round. And this time we shan't have Railus to pave the way for us."

"Or the Controller of the planet," Mexone added soberly.

There was silence again for a moment—a human silence that is. Up above the screaming chaos continued. Watching from the base of the sewer shaft, and comparatively safe because of their depth underground, the five had a vision of hurtling debris and, far away in the one patch of sky that they could see there was a glimpse of a colossal waterspout projecting heavenwards like a mammoth geyser. Evidently part of the oceans themselves being whipped outwards to Zon by the incredibly powerful universal magnetism, which affected all material objects, both metallic and non-metallic.

The five could not be sure but it seemed that the stripping of the planet occupied about two hours. At the end of that time the roaring above gradually ceased, the dark and storm-ridden sky began to clear, and there was a noticeable coldness in the sewer depths together with a tightness about the lungs which told its own tale.

"I think it's over," Abna said at last. "Maybe we'd better go and see."

He waded out of the water to the metal steps and began to climb steadily with the others behind him. He emerged at last into the comparative quietness and coolness, his eyes greeted by a vision similar to that of Karg. Shattered buildings and fallen debris were everywhere, and in several directions fires were burning furiously, sending a vast cloud of smoke over the landscape.

"Well, they've got away with it for the second time," the Amazon said grimly, standing up at Abna's side. "Up to now we're not doing much to justify our existence as Crusaders, I'm afraid."

"Can't blame ourselves for that," Viona shrugged. "We're doing the best we can and nobody can do more."

The Amazon looked bitterly across the waste. In the distance there were the usual survivors, slowly sorting themselves out after the catastrophe that had struck them down.

"Do you suggest we help them?" Abna asked, turning.

"No. At least not directly. They'll manage to work some sort of order out of the chaos. We can best help them by trying to stop further depredations by the Zonians—that is if the Ultra still lies where we left it. We'd better start looking."

The five began moving through the rubble, through the lung-straining air, through the midst of dazed men and women who looked at them with dull eyes and then passed them by. It took them two hours to find the Ultra, moved some distance from its original landing place by the violent perturbations of the air and the effect of the magnetism. Apparently, what had really saved the vessel was the amount of debris on top of it, which had had the effect of anchoring it.

"Start digging," the Amazon ordered, and began to tear with her hands at the small mountain of rubble and metal pieces in which the huge vessel was buried.

Twilight was commencing to fall before they had at last dug a tunnel through the rubbish wide enough to admit of their bodies. After that it was an easy matter to enter the control room. The Amazon switched on the bright lights and glanced at the piled-up rubbish outside the windows.

"Well, are we ready for departure to the next neighbor planet?" she asked, after a while.

"We're ready," Abna said, "but whether we'll be in time or not is open to doubt. The Zonians will probably be watching space to see if there's any signs of the Ultra on the move—and the moment they see us heading to one of the neighbor worlds they'll speed things up to produce a repetition of what's happened here. There seems little doubt anymore but what we're a bait for them."

"In that I agree," the Amazon sighed. "But I don't see what else we can do. Even if we make the Ultra invisible they'll still be able to detect its presence with instruments, so that isn't any advantage."

Abna thought for a moment, then: "Let's look at the position. We know we're being watched and that the Zonians will attack wherever they see us, in the hope of destroying us, which they know their fleet cannot do. That means we're certain of getting an attack on whatever planet we choose to visit: we're no longer in doubt as to where they'll strike. Right?"

"So it would seem," the Amazon assented, and the others nodded.

Abna continued: "Our difficulty seems to be one of time. Though we assume the Zonians will want a slight interval to gather their forces together again, we don't know it as a fact. They may be able to make quite a quick turn-around—far more quickly than we can build our intended repulsive system, considering all the initial details we'll have to contend with—"

"Meaning, more plainly, that we just haven't time to erect the repulsive system no matter how hard we try or how fast we move?" Viona asked, and Abna gave a grave nod.

"That would seem to be the answer. The Zonians are too quick for us. There are two worlds still untouched in this system, ready and open to be attacked. How can we get to one or other of them and devise something that will give us assured safety?"

There was a thoughtful pause, broken at length by Thania.

"As yet," she said, half apologetically, "I am not thoroughly experienced in the ways of the Crusaders, therefore I hesitate to make a suggestion... Just the same, I have one."

"Such as?" the Amazon asked.

"Well it does seem to me, as a looker-on, that you are devoting more attention to a complicated scheme than a simple one. You want to build a repulsive system, which will take a long time. Time in which the Accursed Ones will beat you to it. There's an easier way than that."

"There is?" Abna looked at her in surprise.

"As a matter of fact Mexone gave me the original idea," Thania proceeded, glancing towards him. "He said something not very long ago about the Zonians being completely eliminated."

"That's right," Mexone confirmed. "But I used the term in a general sense. We hope eventually that not a single Zonian will remain alive."

"That, I think, is within our reach to accomplish..." Thania's eyes had brightened with sudden excitement. "It may mean the devastation of yet another world as a bait—that we can't avoid, but it will mean that the fourth world in the system will never be attacked because there won't be a Zonian left to do it."

"Why won't there?" The Amazon was staring at her.

"I am thinking of high-powered nuclear bombs," the girl said. "We have them, and you know what they are and their tremendous destructiveness. The Zonian magnetism drags everything from the surface of a planet—that we know. Buildings, people, oceans, and air. Suppose it also drew a quantity of nuclear bombs as well? Suppose the entire stockpile of bombs owned by my world, Karg, and the one remaining neighbor we choose to visit, are arranged at a convenient point on the surface of the neighbor world we travel to, with the firing mechanism open and ready for action? What will happen? These bombs will be drawn back to Zon along with everything else, but when they arrive they'll explode. And if there are several thousand of them, which there will be, Zon will be in a pretty sorry state when they have all exploded."

There was an amazed silence for a moment, silence chiefly because the girl had suggested so simple and yet so devastating a plan. Finally it was Abna who spoke.

"I can't think why the girl isn't right. Vi!" he exclaimed, turning to the Amazon. "These scientists are always anxious to steal everything, so there's no reason why they shouldn't have bombs as well, and all that goes with them. Just retribution indeed!"

"And they'll certainly land," Thania added, "because to have their magnetism working, and receive stolen air and water, their own protective screen will have to be out of action. Up to now, as I understand it, that has been the one thing that has balked your efforts. With the Zero-Thought Amplifier, for instance."

"Yes, that's true enough," the Amazon agreed: then she fell to thought, seeking as usual for flaws in the plan. She was still astonished at its simplicity: it demanded examination from all angles to see if there were any flaws.

"Why," she asked presently, "have not any bombs been sucked away from Karg, or from this planet?"

"That's not a difficult question to answer," the girl said. "Being in a Government office—prior to teaming up with you, I mean—I know exactly where our stockpile of nuclear bombs was kept—and that was deep underground in special chambers. They were there in case of any hostile action at any time… Well, you know how little the magnetism affected us at the bottom of that sewer well, and we were not protected by a vault as the bombs are. That's why they were safe, being so far below surface. I expect the same conditions apply here."

"It will take an enormous number of even nuclear bombs to destroy an entire planet," Mexone said.

"That depends on the power of them," the Amazon answered. "We can soon test one and find how efficient it is, then we'll |have a good idea of the cumulative effect. If it comes to that we have a stock of nuclear bombs aboard the Ultra at this very moment, but their power isn't great enough to produce the widespread damage we're hoping for."

"If some of the Zonians should escape the onslaught they've brought on themselves, they'll still have to fight the fallout and ruin of radioactive dust that will plague them for years to come… What I mean is they'll be finished as a race of killers so far as this system is concerned. And I should think it would add the final touch if the survivors of Karg, this world, and the planet we elect to visit next, were to take over the metal world which the Zonians have so nicely prepared with their stolen air and oceans. That would, in my view, be justice in its highest sense."

The Amazon began to smile as she glimpsed the possibilities.

"Finally," Thania said slowly, "those who take over the metal world will be able to organize themselves fully against attack by the Zonians, which in any case can't amount to much with so few—if any—survivors and their scanty scientific resources."

"Thania," the Amazon said slowly, putting an arm about her slim shoulders, "I think you have the answer. Strange indeed how we get into the way of thinking out the most complicated things, when actually simplicity is the answer." She glanced through the window onto the debris and tangled ruin beyond. "From the look of things we shan't be able to get any sense out of anybody on this planet for a long tine to come. We'd better try your own world first—if you, happen to know where the stockpile of bombs is kept?"

The girl nodded. "Yes, I know. It may take a little while to find than with all the landmarks blasted out of recognition, but we'll do it somehow."

"And if the Zonians trace us to Karg?" Abna questioned. "What then?"

"I should think they most certainly will," Viona commented. "From the way things are it looks as though they have us under observation all the time."

"We'll just have to risk it," the Amazon shrugged. "I don't think they'll try further magnetism against Karg just because we happen to be there—and even if they do we'll defeat it somehow as we did here. The real trouble will come when we go to the next neighbor world, which at present hasn't been touched. Then there'll be an attack, I imagine."

"Which will seal the Zonians' death warrant," Abna said.

"Exactly." The Amazon turned to the switchboard. "Well, let's be off. There's nothing to be gained by delay."

She closed the airlock, switched on the power plant, and then stood watching as the huge vessel tore free of the ruin around it and shot skywards. Once in the void she set the course directly for Karg and then looked beyond the ravaged planet to where Zon hung like a speck in the firmament.

"Our unpleasant friends seem to be busy," she commented. "Evidently consolidating what they have gained from Biuz. Have a look."

The others did not need telling. From the windows they could see what the Amazon meant. Stretching across from the world of Zon to a distant gray speck in the void was a thin, nebulous kind of bridge, visible because of the intense clarity of vision in absolute space.

Abna said finally: "I suppose that's Biuz's stolen air and water being projected to the metal world?"

"I imagine so," the Amazon agreed, her face set. "Perhaps it's just as well they're so completely occupied. It will take the heat off us for a while."

CHAPTER 9

Atomic vengeance

Whether or not the Zonians were keeping a watch on space, nothing happened to the Ultra during her multi-million mile trip back to Karg. They landed without incident close to the makeshift town with its huddles of people and little campfires. But this time the people made no effort to come and see what the visitation was about. They had already seen the Ultra land once and depart again with the unfortunate Railus, so they evidently assumed that there was no reason for them to investigate.

"Naturally," Thania said, "we shall have to do all our own carrying even when we've located the bombs. You realize that?"

"We're ready for it," the Amazon smiled. "I should imagine that will be the least of our troubles. We've got to locate them first."

Thania stepped outside into the thin air and sunlight as the airlock opened and stood trying to get her bearings. The others came to her aide and waited as she weighed things up.

"The city center was here," she murmured. "The main street cane down this way and branched off into the Fifth Intersection. Then there were the laboratories and executive offices—" She broke off into murmuring to herself. "That means, as far as I can tell, that the stockpile vaults should be—about there."

She indicated a stretch where girders, mangled and twisted, still stood, surrounded by great mountains of stone and metal.

"Yes, that was originally the Central Bank," she went on. "The bomb stockpile was underneath the bank."

"Under the bank?" Abna raised his eyebrows. "Rather a funny place to keep bombs, isn't it?"

Thania hesitated, then she smiled. "Oh, I see what you mean. I don't mean it was a money bank: it was a bank for keeping weapons of defense. A—er—what you call an armory."

"That's different," the Amazon said. "All right, we'll see what we can find. We'll need tools from the Ultra, and from the look of things there's plenty of digging ahead."

In that she was certainly right. The digging occupied nearly two hours of hard work, even for the iron-muscled Crusaders, before they finally bared a layer of a layer of metal—a great flat sheet of it on which their picks and shovels rang noisily. When they came to this stage Thania stopped and wiped her face and forehead with the back of her hand.

"I was right," she said in delight. "This is the roof of the underground vault. We'll have to get through it somehow."

"I'll get the disintegrator," Abna said, and in a few minutes had done so. After that, it was only a matter of moments to bore a hole large enough to admit of their bodies. This done, they dropped below into complete darkness. But it did not stay dark for long as five atomic torches cast a fan of brilliance about the place.

It was quite big, with metal walls on every side. Also a door with a combination lock, which of course they hadn't needed to battle with since they had come through the roof—or rather the ceiling. Originally a massive building had been poised on the metal roof, gone now like everything else into ruin and chaos.

"There!" Thania said, pointing to row after row of metal racks set into the walls. "Those are the bombs."

The others went closer and looked at them. They were like gray pears, clipped round the neck with clamps which themselves were fastened into the racks. Interested, the Amazon went closer and pulled one of them free, examining it carefully, particularly the timing and switch mechanism on the neck.

"That's the vital part," Thania said, coming to her side. "You can do anything you like with the bombs, even drop them if you wish—but they won't explode with that mechanism being set. And that's something that's beyond me. I don't know how it works."

"We'll soon figure it out aboard the Ultra," the Amazon responded. "First we've got to transport every one of these, and the sooner the bettor. So let's get started."

Thereupon the task began, and it lasted far into the evening and the night, under the cold stars and the last of the twinkling campfires the five kept up their task—the Amazon and Abna working below, and Viona, Mexone, and Thania up above, doing the transporting and stacking the bombs neatly in one of the Ultra's huge storage holds.

There was a hold up when they devised—and manufactured with the machine tools—racks to hold the bombs steady, otherwise everything went according to plan. So finally the job was done and the Ultra took off into space again, the richer by nearly five hundred bombs.

Once in space, the Crusaders rested, had a meal, and recovered from their exertions in the thin air. It was then that the Amazon made an announcement as to the next moves.

"We'll deal with Biuz next, and hope we have the same immunity from attack as we've had so far. It might be a good idea in between, Abna, for us to figure out how the firing mechanism works. As for rest of you I would suggest you get some sleep whilst you have the chance. We'll keep the Ultra on slow speed: that will mean we'll take longer to make the journey and it will give the survivors of Biuz a better chance to have got themselves organized."

Her plan was adopted without comment; then she and Abna set to work with one of the bombs on the control room table. With lenses they carefully examined the firing and timing mechanism, calmly disregarding the fact that they had before them a bomb that could blow them and the Ultra clean out of the Milky Way if they made the slightest miscalculation.

"Not a very difficult matter," the Amazon said finally. "Pull this lever down here, set the timer for 'Now' or whatever future time we wish, and there you are. In regard to our own requirements, we'll have to set the bombs at 'Now' which means they will be all set to fire themselves the moment they hit Zon's surface. And a mighty explosion there'll be when this lot arrives," she finished with a grim smile.

"I'm wondering," Abna reflected, "if we need any more bombs from Biuz and the next planet we're intending to visit. After all, five hundred nuclear bombs is an enormous number, and I'd say quite enough to shatter the surface civilization of any planet completely."

"We could make a test," the Amazon said. "Eject something into outer space and fire one of these bombs after it."

"Good idea," Abna agreed, and rose—then when he reached the observation window he gave a start. Turning, he said dryly, "I have the feeling that we're going to make a bomb test sooner than we expected, Vi! That is, if our friends out here start trying to attack us—otherwise we won't feel justified."

The Amazon joined him at the window. She too gave a slight start as she beheld a dozen spaceships of Zon pursuing the Ultra.

"We've missed our chance of striking whilst the magnetic shield was lifted to let those ships out," she sighed. "Well, can't be helped now... What's their intention, do you think? Our destruction?"

"I can't think what else."

Abna had hardly replied before the radio buzzed for attention. He gave the Amazon a glance, switched in the Language Translator, then snapped the main switch on the radio controls.

"Yes?" he questioned curtly. "Abna, of the Crusaders speaking."

There was a pause, then a harsh, unsentimental voice responded.

"Your movements from planet to planet have been kept under close observation. We have done so ever since you killed Commander Nio and put his fleet to rout. Perhaps you have to be reminded that a state of war exists between Zon and the planet Karg?"

"And the planet Biuz as well, judging from what you've done to it!" Abna snapped. "As for ourselves, we shall continue to come and go as we please and have no intention of being ordered about by you... Over."

"Very well—but you are very foolish. We are armed as Commander Nio never was, and we shall attack you with everything we have got. Remember that there are no rules in war—or at least none that we choose to recognize. You will be destroyed—completely!"

"If you are wise," Abna said, "you will immediately retreat as did the fleet of Commander Nio. You have no idea of the forces you are up against."

"They cannot be greater those of Zon!"

With a contemptuous movement Abna switched off the radio and looked at the Amazon. She was smiling cynically.

"Evidently our egotistical friends need teaching a lesson," she said, shrugging. "And since they're determined to perpetuate a state of war we've nothing to blame ourselves for... Here goes."

She picked up the bomb from the table, adjusted the timing mechanism to 'Now' and then pulled over the firing pin. Crossing to the ejector mechanism with the bomb in her hand she surveyed the setup outside. The fleet was converging into a nearby group, ready no doubt to pool resources in an onslaught on the Ultra. What they were planning to do did not concern the Amazon. The main point was that the twelve space machines were in line with the trajectory the nuclear bomb would take when fired from the ejector.

"Two birds with one stone," the Amazon said, laying the bomb carefully in the ejector trap. "We can test the bomb and destroy them at the same time."

With that she pressed the ejector mechanism's button, then immediately she and Abna jumped to the window to watch what happened, first taking the precaution of donning protective goggles. They found out almost immediately as striking the first ship in the fleet, the bomb exploded. And the violence of it was almost unbelievable.

There was a momentary flash of intolerable blue-white light from which the Amazon and Abna jerked their eyes quickly; then came the soundless shock waves, pitching even the huge Ultra up and down as though the vessel were in a stormy sea. The force of the explosion must have been colossal—for all twelve of the ships crumbled and split beneath its impact, spewing helpless Zonian engineers into the merciless void... Smoke and drifting metal, to say nothing of volatized bodies, filled the entire area for a time—then at last the smoke had dispersed and there nothing but wreckage and cosmic dust drawing gently together under the common law of attraction.

"Whew!" Abna commented. "If that's what one bomb can do we certainly don't need any more to augment our present five hundred odd. We've seen atomic and other nuclear bombs before but never anything with a force like that."

The Amazon nodded grimly, then she turned as Viona, Thania, and Mexone came hurrying into the control room, dressing gowns thrown hastily over their sleep attire.

"What happened?" Viona asked in surprise. "I was just enjoying pleasant dreams when I was nearly thrown out of bed by a shock of some kind. Somebody attacking us?"

"The Zonians had such an idea," the Amazon responded, "but I think they've been taught a lesson. Have a look through the window and see what only one Kargian bomb can do."

Viona looked—and so did Mexone and Thania. They turned back into the control room with amazed faces.

"One bomb only did that?" Viona asked, astonished.

"Right," the Amazon confirmed. "Amongst that wreckage were twelve of Zon's proudest ships, armed to the teeth. Your father and I had just worked out how to handle the bomb mechanism when the Zonians outside made some ridiculous demands upon us. They got their answer—and if Zon persists in attacking the other worlds as they have Karg and Biuz they'll draw down extinction on themselves. Anyway, it's up to them."

"Come to think of it," Mexone said, "we'd better be careful we don't have too many bombs to be drawn away—considering the violence of this one—"

"We're not bothering with any more than the five hundred we have already," the Amazon said. "We had just decided on that. So our next stop will not be at Biuz but the planet beyond that."

"Where we'll lay the nuclear eggs?" Viona asked.

"Exactly, once we have established communication with the people and explained our purpose."

"That being as it is," Viona said, "I'll go and catch up on my beauty sleep. Coming, Mex?"

She left the control room with Mexone and Thania following behind her. Abna glanced across the Amazon as she stood pensively by the window, obviously trying to sort something out in her mind.

"Can I help?" Abna asked, and at that the Amazon came to attention.

"Yes, Abna, I think you can. I was just thinking— To gain our purpose with these five hundred bombs a planet has to be sacrificed, hasn't it?"

He nodded. "I'm afraid you're right, Vi. They'll have to drawn away with everything else when the next planet is attacked—and that will presumably be the one we'll visit next."

Abna looked out of the window at the planet in question, gleaming as a solitary point beyond Biuz. And further again, on the rim of the system, was the final planet in the system.

"The civilization of the planet we intend to visit doesn't really mean anything since it can be rebuilt," the Amazon mused. "What I'm trying to work out is how we can warn the people of the planet to escape before we plant the bombs—for sure enough the magnetism will soon follow once we're seen to have landed, particularly so since we gave that second fleet such a trouncing."

"The minute we land on the planet the danger signal goes up, eh?" Abna asked. "Yes, you're right enough there. Well, what about warning the people? Can anything be done with radio on a closed circuit?"

"Yes," the Amazon said finally. "It's an idea worth trying, Abna. In fact that's the only method we can properly use which the Zonians won't be able to pick up..." She thought on swiftly.

"I think the best idea would probably be to fly away into space beyond this system, to give the impression we're leaving it and going into outer space. When we're out of range of the Zonian detectors we'll come back, invisibly, approaching our intended planet from its far side."

"Detectors can still pick us up again, invisible or otherwise."

"Truly, but we're going to try a little bluff. Once the Zonians think we've departed they'll probably not be on the lookout and won't have any detectors in operation."

"We're still defeating our own purpose," Abna sighed. "The Zonians are not likely to attack the planet we're contacting unless they see we're landing on it. At least they're not likely to attack for a very long time when they think we're out of the way."

The Amazon said patiently, "We shall warn the people and give them a chance to get away—then we'll make the Ultra visible and land in the ordinary way. Once we've made the people safe we'll be able to take care of ourselves."

Abna reflected for a while and then gave a nod. "Okay, we can try it and see what happens."

The Amazon turned to the switchboard and increased the speed so that the Ultra fled with ever mounting velocity into the endless deeps, apparently fleeing the system...

* * * *

The journey into space and then back again took four weeks—purposely, time in which the Amazon felt sure the Zonians would cease to watch their detectors—and by this time she and the others knew exactly what they were going to do. The Amazon operated switches that caused the walls, floor, and roof of the Ultra to mist and the ship to take on the appearance of glass. Against the black of space it was virtually invisible. When eventually they came back to within a million miles of shattered Biuz's interplanetary neighbor they were all set for action… Cruising around the busy, thriving planet, the Ultra still hidden by invisibility the Amazon made radio contact with the Language Translator in action.

"Golden Amazon of the Cosmic Crusaders calling the next world to Biuz…" And she kept on sending the recorded message until there at last came an answer.

"Message received, Golden Amazon. Identify your position and from where you are speaking. You are not unknown to us. Over."

The Amazon raised her eyebrows in surprise as she took hold of the microphone.

"Not unknown to you? Can you elaborate on that statement? Over."

"We have recently established radio contact with Biuz to inquire as to the nature of the catastrophe that recently struck them. The surviving scientists told us of the attack by the Accursed Ones, and also told us of your efforts to prevent he occurrence. We salute your efforts, Golden Amazon and Crusaders, and we wish to know why you desire to have contact with us. Repeat: will you kindly identify your position as we request, so we may trace you with our telescopes? Over."

"It would be folly to do that," the Amazon said. "We are a million miles from you and that is all I am going to tell you. If we reveal ourselves it will only be a matter of time before the Zonians will bring disaster down on you as they did on Biuz. Listen carefully whilst I explain the circumstances…"

When the Amazon had given all the details the voice replied: "You have devised a very effective scheme, Amazon. That is not just the opinion of myself—I am purely the director of radio communication for this planet—but the opinion of all the government heads who are grouped around me and who have heard your words through the loud speaker. We gather then that you suggest nothing less than our exodus into space? Over."

"There is no other way," the Amazon answered. "You can see for yourselves that, even if we had not intervened, the Zonians will turn their magnetism on you sooner or later. Over."

"That seems to be inevitable, yes—but unhappily we are not the masters of space travel. Nor are our friends on the one remaining world on the outskirts of this system. Space travel has been mastered by the Accursed Ones, and by the inhabitants of Karg and Biuz—

but not by us. Whatever contacts we have made have been by radio, or else they have visited us. Not unnaturally, they have kept their priceless space traveling secret to themselves... Obviously we cannot evacuate our world of Tron as you, suggest because we haven't the transport—and even if we had it would take a long time and vast resources to carry millions of people. Over."

The Amazon switched off the microphone for a moment and gave Abna a dismayed glance.

"This is something we never thought of, Abna. Fools that we've been! We assumed they have space travel and it was an assumption which we had no right to make."

Abna moved forward thoughtfully. "Let me talk them for a moment. We're not finished yet. I've got an idea—a risky one, but it might work."

The Amazon moved to one side and Abna took over her place. He switched the microphone on again.

"Listen, my friends, to what I have to say. I am Abna, the male leader of the Crusaders. Since you have no space travel you, can't evacuate, and those planets who have got it—Biuz and Karg—are so completely shattered they cannot help. Right—what other scientific facilities have you? Have you the resources to build a series of towers at various points on your planet? Towers that will give forth an aura of magnetism to protect your world? Over."

"We have immense engineering resources, Abna, and could gear up those resources to infinite expansion if need be—but what do you mean by an aura of magnetism? Over."

Abna said: "The issue is simply this. The Zonians throw magnetism against you, don't they? If you generate the same magnetism you automatically deflect their efforts on the principle of like charges repelling each other. You understand that? Over."

"Yes, we understand. But how are we to know the kind of magnetism the Zonians will use against us? Over."

"You will know it in detail, because we shall give it to you. It has been part of our campaign against the Zonians to find out the type of magnetism they use, and so far we have not been able to make use of our information. Now we can do so—and will do so. I will give you the formula now if you will listen..." and for the next ten minutes Abna lost himself in a maze of mathematical findings. Then he switched back to Tron for their comments.

"We have all the details, Abna, and must congratulate you on the exactness of your computations. The only point we don't understand is how this will help you to place your nuclear bombs. It will be no use placing them on our planet if we're in a position to deflect the magnetism. Over."

Abna said: "We shan't use your planet, my friend. We have other ideas. What I want to know is how quickly you can erect and equip those towers? Over."

"It will take about four weeks of time. Over."

"Then start immediately. For the period you've mentioned we'll depart again into a far region of space and not give our ever watchful Zonians a chance to detect us. We'll radio again when the time has elapsed and see how you are progressing. Over."

"Suppose, Abna, that the Zonians attack the outer world first? How can they be saved? Over."

"I'm one hundred percent sure hat they will attack your world before the outer one, my friend, and I say that because we shall be the bait… Now do as I have requested and let nothing stand in your way to get those towers erected and equipped as soon as possible. Good luck! Over and out."

Abna switched off and turned to the control board. He started the Ultra moving slowly away into the outer space away from the system, then he turned to find the eyes of the Amazon, Viona, Mexone and Thania fixed on him, full of questions.

"What," the Amazon asked pointedly, "are you driving at? Where do we fit into things now? What happens to the bombs?"

"They fall on Zon as planned—eventually," Abna grinned.

"Stop being evasive and explain yourself!"

"All right. The engineers on Tron build their towers for the magnetism whilst we're away. The Zonians won't do anything before then—at least it's very unlikely that they will. That will start when we return to a position near Tron. The position will be dead between Tron and Zon, at which position we shall become fully visible. Then we—"

"Wait a minute," the Amazon said quickly. "I think I get your idea. Because we're near Tron, the Zonians will release their magnetism with the idea of killing two birds with one stone. Since we'll be in the track of their magnetic beam when they aim it at Tron they'll be under the impression that they'll strip the planet and absorb us in the magnetism at the same time. Is that it?"

"That's it: we'll be the proverbial red rag to a bull. Only it won't work out quite that way. For one thing the magnetism will be deflected when it hits Tron and, we hope, won't have any effect. For another, the beam which is also embracing us won't drag us to Zon—we'll fight against it with a triple power plant as before—which means that the only thing the Zonians will draw through space back onto themselves will be the five hundred nuclear bombs which will smash Zon to pieces when they arrive. Being so small they'll never be seen coming, and once they land the magnetism we'll have to fight against will cease."

The Amazon moved slowly, her brows knitted. "I can visualize everything you've said, Abna, except the matter of how the bombs get to Zon when they're inside the storage hold."

"They're there now, admitted, but they won't be. Each one will have its firing mechanism set for instant action, and each on will be put on the outside of the vessel—on the roof probably. A simple rail will keep them together and they'll stay on and with the Ultra for as long as we wish, held by the law of mass attraction. They'll only move when the magnetism draws them away... Understand?"

The Amazon took a deep breath. "Completely! It's a marvelous idea, Abna."

"And not without its dangers," Viona pointed out. "Once those bombs are set to fire and piled in readiness on the Ultra's exterior, we have to remember that the slightest jar or shock will explode them—and if that happens we can say goodbye."

"It won't," Abna said confidently. "Whoever heard of a jar or a shock in infinite space?"

"Finally," the Amazon said, "we shall have to trust to luck that the Zonians don't attack the outermost planet first."

Abna shrugged. "If they do, it's just hard luck on the people of the last planet, that's all. We've done all we can—and I'm still confident that the Zonians won't do anything at all for the time being—until they see we're in the picture. Then they'll act good and fast—and in so doing will sign their own death warrant."

The Amazon relaxed. "Well, that's settled. And we've got four weeks to kill. We'd better start thinking up ways and means to pass the time..."

Abna said: "Fixing the timing and firing mechanism on those

bombs won't be such a light task. We might as well begin it while we're cruising around and then we'll have all our arrangements ready for when the great moment comes…"

** * * ***

Moving at a leisurely speed, the Ultra finally drifted so far into the deeps of the Milky Way that the Zonian system of worlds was entirely lost to sight—but not its sun. This remained as a point of return, a golden glowing star pinpointed on instruments so there could be no mistake when it came to making the return trip.

Meanwhile the Crusaders set about the task of preparing their 'surprise packet' for the ruthless Zonians. Day by day, and week by week—checked entirely by the chronometers since there was neither day nor night in the accepted sense—they prepared the bombs for action, a frighteningly dangerous task that demanded all their care and steadiness.

And as each bomb was made 'live' by Viona, Mexone, and Thania it was transferred through the roof trap to Abna and the Amazon, working in spacesuits on the Ultra's exterior to stack the bombs in readiness. They worked on the job at intervals, carefully stacking the gray 'pears' within a loose rack, so that they could be whipped away without hindrance when the magnetism struck them.

An exacting and nerve-racking job with only the everlasting stars and distant blazing nebulae for their surroundings, otherwise there was nothing but eternal space. Each knew that they worked with instant death in their thickly gauntleted hands if they chanced to make a mistake, or stumble in their magnetic boots… Half an hour at a time was all they could trust themselves to do, then they had to return below for relaxation and the recovery of their nerve.

Meticulously careful though they had to be, they did the job finally and were rewarded by seeing the 'live' bombs stacked in the rack. A terrible cargo beyond doubt, and one that they would never have used themselves. If the Zonians again reached out with greed and theft as their main impetus, they would bring death down on their own heads, which was exactly as it should be according to the Crusaders' reckoning.

And finally the four weeks were up. From a hardly moving position in the distant void, the Ultra began to gather speed—but gently, as the bomb load was remembered. Mirrors reflecting the scene outside showed that the bombs were motionless, held of course by the mass of the Ultra itself and bound by common law to move at the same velocity as it did. And there was no jarring or friction, both unknown qualities in deep space unless they were the outcome of some fortuity or other.

"Nevertheless," the Amazon, murmured, as they came within a million miles of Tron once again, "I'll be mighty thankful when we've rid ourselves of our load of eggs…"

She glanced through the observation window and then gave a sigh of relief. Tron looked exactly as it had done before: there were no signs of its having been ravaged by magnetic beams as yet.

"And from the look of things," Abna said, studying the scene through the high power telescope, "they've got those towers built all right. I can see six of then on the side of the planet facing us… Good! It looks as though we'll be able to lay our eggs in good time, Vi."

He left the telescope and crossed over to the radio. He switched in the Language Translator and then spoke. Within a few moments a voice answered.

"I am receiving you clearly, Abna of the Crusaders. For my own people I have only to report that the twelve towers have been built at strategic points on all points of Tron, so arranged that they will surround our planet with a shell of magnetic repulsion whenever you give the signal. Over."

Abna said quietly: "I am giving that signal now, my friend. Whilst we have been absent we have made our arrangements with regard to the bombs, and we go forth now to bait the enemy. I am convinced that he will attack you and us simultaneously, so be prepared… Whatever may happen, keep a watch on the proceedings with your telescope. If Zon is destroyed, as we think it will be, you will quickly be aware of the fact. Afterwards, when all this is over, you can do one thing for my colleagues and myself as recompense for what we have done for you. Over."

"Anything, friend Abna, that may be within our power. Over."

"You will radio Karg and Biuz, pay them our respects, and tell then that a world awaits them where they can build again without fear. I refer to the gray metal world which the Zonians have created, and for which they have stolen air and water. We would send the message ourselves, but it is possible that our last great struggle may hurl us out of this system entirely and we shall not attempt to come back. You will do that? Over."

"We will do that, yes. And may the gods watch over you in this battle of yours. Our eternal thanks and thoughts go with you. Over and out."

Abna clicked the radio switch and compressed his lips. He looked at the others tensely.

"This is it, then?" the Amazon asked quietly.

"Yes—when we're sure they've got that magnetism going on Tron." Abna looked out the window and then glanced at the detectors on the switchboard. It was not long before Tron became suffused with pale lavender color and the instruments on the switchboard, directed towards the planet, gave a reading which showed a high magnetic intensity.

"Okay—they're protected," Abna said.

"Suppose," Thania remarked, "the Zonians see that pale violet color over the planet? Will they suspect anything?"

"Possibly, but they'll most likely regard it as innocuous. That is usually the reaction of the egotistical. Anyway, we're ready to become the decoy, Vi."

The Amazon nodded, thought for a moment of the load of death on he roof of the vessel, and then steered the huge ship in the direction of Zon, so many millions of miles away. When at last the navigation readings showed that the vessel was in a direct line between Zon and Tron she pulled the switch which gave the Ultra visibility once more, as well as cutting down speed.

"Up to them now," she said, as the others congregated round her, all of them tensely expectant. "We can do nothing but wait—and watch."

"You're ready for the magnetism?" Abna asked, and the Amazon nodded.

"Completely. I've got the power plant controls set in reverse so I can throw them the moment there's trouble…"

"And you three know your tasks?" Abna looked at Viona, Mexone, and Thania, as they quickly nodded.

"We're all ready," Viona said. "We stand by to replace fuses if and when they go."

"Good…" Abna looked at the spare copper blocks for tripling the energy of the power plant is need be. "We're okay—a sitting pigeon apparently, but the most dangerous pigeon any scientists of any world ever encountered."

Silence. The Ultra drifted very slightly in the motions of space. Abna turned the magnetic detectors towards Zon and left them positioned there. As yet they gave a zero reading.

"At least they'll give us a few seconds warning," he said. "And that's all. The magnetism will flash across space at the speed of light when it does come."

The Amazon made no comment. She glanced once at Tron and beheld the protection of the lavender-hued repulsive magnetism still there. She thought of the assembled bombs on the Ultra's roof. Then she looked at far distant Karg, Biuz, and finally Zon—a solitary yellow planet, glowing with a molten gold light that seemed somehow to bespeak the evil quality of its inhabitants—

The chronometer flicked through the seconds, steady and remorseless. Half an hour passed. An hour. Then—

"Look out!" Abna exclaimed suddenly. "The instruments are reacting..."

He had hardly time to make the announcement before things happened. Through the window there was a bright core of brilliance making itself evident as a projection from Zon. Moving with the incredible speed of light it was across the gulf in seconds, engulfing the Ultra in a lavender-lighted blaze and hurtling after that straight for the world of Tron. What happened there the Crusaders had not time to observe: they had enough to do inside the Ultra.

Caught by the magnetic beam the ship suddenly started to move with rising acceleration towards Zon. Abna remained by the window, staring intently outside—then he gave a whoop of delight as he saw a mass of gray specks hurtling ahead of the Ultra drawn irresistibly by magnetic force, and because the bombs were smaller and had less mass they traveled far faster than the Ultra's huge bulk.

The power plant suddenly came into action. Whining shrilly in reverse, and—as on that other occasion—the Amazon strove with a slow increase of power to turn the huge vessel aside out of the stream. And again, as before, the power plant was not up to the struggle demanded of it.

"Have all the bombs gone?" the Amazon demanded, and Abna glanced at her from by the window.

"A lot of them have. I can't be sure— Hey, Thania, what are you doing?" he broke off in amazement, as he saw the girl struggling quickly into a spacesuit.

"Only one way to find if the bombs have gone, and that's go and look," she grinned, snapping the fastenings on her suit.

"If you go out there you'll be snatched away in the beam," Abna shouted, rushing over to her. "Listen to me, can't you—"

Since Abna's words were drowned out by the scream of the power plant—and also because Thania was putting her helmet on—she did not hear a word. She raced out of the control room before anybody could stop her and fled through the main passage way. Instantly, Abna, Viona and Mexone were after her—but they arrived a few seconds too late to grab her. The door of the air-chamber slammed in their faces and they could only watch in horror through the glass panel as the youngster quickly climbed the metal ladder to the roof and pushed up the huge trap.

The view of her was extraordinary, silhouetted against a violet haze from the beam, which in itself blotted out the stars. She climbed up a few rungs of the ladder, looked along the surface of the Ultra's roof, and then climbed down again. She shut the trapdoor and reopened the slide door of the air chamber.

"You reckless little idiot!" Abna snorted, when she had pulled offer her helmet. "Do you realize that you could have been pulled out of that manhole like a cork out of a bottle?"

She grinned impishly. "I could have if I'd climbed right onto the roof—not otherwise," she smiled. "Don't worry, Abna, I'm getting to know all the tricks. Anyway, I've seen enough. Every bomb has gone—"

"Abna!" came the Amazon's distraught voice from the control room. "Put more copper in the power plant—"

Abna dived along the passageway, the roar of the power plant dinning in his ears as he entered the control room.

"Bombs all gone," he said. "Thania's checked on it. That reckless kid's going to give us all heart failure before she's finished."

Thania came in, dragging her spacesuit and scooping the tumbled blonde hair from her face. The Amazon only glanced at her.

"Nice work," she said briefly. "You're a girl after my own heart, Thania. Bombs all gone, you say?"

"Yes. Every one of them."

"Good!" The Amazon's eyes gleamed. "Now I can maneuver in a bit more comfort—and to get out of this magnetism I'll certainly have to maneuver to good effect. If we get dragged back to Zon behind the bombs as they explode— Whew!"

Abna snapped off the power, put in the extra copper cubes, and then snapped the power on again. Immediately Viona, Mexone, and Thania took up their positions behind the fuses, ready to go into action the second they were needed.

As on that other occasion the struggle was severe. The fuses blew time and again and the Ultra lost precious ground as the fuses were rapidly replaced. The Amazon struggled with the controls, and although there was a reading of maximum power, in the immense tug-of-war between the Ultra and the magnetism, there was no doubt that the magnetism was slowly winning.

"I don't think," the Amazon whispered, "that we're going to make it in time. They've got a terrific pull this time: even greater than last—"

Abruptly her words ceased. Looking through the window with the others she saw a flash from distant Zon—a brilliant blue-white flash. It was followed immediately by another; then suddenly the entire universe seemed to blaze with incredible flame as Zon was transformed from a planet into what looked like a first magnitude star.

"We've done it!" Viona cried in delight. "The bombs have got there—some of them anyway. They must have traveled at a terrific speed."

"Nearly that of light with the magnetism as strong as it is," the Amazon said tensely.

"Yet the power's still on—the magnetism, I mean," Mexone said, puzzling. "With the planet destroyed you'd think it would stop—"

"It will," Abna said confidently. "Don't forget the distance. A few seconds have to elapse before—"

He got no further. Suddenly the pull from doomed Zon stopped dead. Immediately the enormous pull of the Ultra in the reverse direction had the effect of flinging the five to the floor, exactly as had been the case before when they had played tag with the magnetism.

But this time the Amazon had made preparations. As the velocity of the ship steadily increased under the action of the triple power plant, pre-set controls operated to plunge the Ultra into hyperspace. The acceleration ceased, and the Amazon found herself floating weightless into the upper reaches of the control room, the others somersaulting and gyrating weirdly around her.

She smiled, pulled herself to the floor by gripping the switchboard projections, and then snapped over switches. The stabilizers responded gradually, and the five floated gently back to the floor as conditions became normal. Within a few seconds, normal gravity had been restored.

"Nice work," Abna commented. "I suggest we have a meal as we continue cruising in hyperspace until we've covered a dozen or so light-years—sufficient to put us in reach of another solar system. Then we'll drop into normal space and see where we've ended up, and more particularly, whether anything merits our investigation."

It was some three hours later when the Amazon operated the controls that caused the Ultra to drop out of hyperspace and re-enter normal space. During that interval the Ultra had exceeded the speed of light by many times, and as a consequence, when Abna moved to the window and gazed out onto the deeps of space there was no trace of Zon—or even of any planet in the system. Following its huge leap through hyperspace the Ultra had taken a shortcut across several light years of normal space, and was—now that it was again in the normal space-time continuum—hurtling through the void at a steady velocity of about a quarter of the speed of light.

"Just as well I told them on Tron that we wouldn't be back," Abna commented, relaxing. "Well, I think we can truthfully say it was a job well done."

"Beyond doubt," the Amazon agreed, joining him along with the others. "And our good wishes for the future go with those people of Tron, Karg, Biuz, and the outermost world…"

For a moment there was silence. It was broken finally by Thania.

"Well?" she asked brightly. What do we do next? This is a grand life as long as there's something happening. When there isn't anything it must get pretty dull."

"That's what I think," Viona said, with an impish smile.

The Amazon sighed and glanced at Abna, "Even if we could get old, Abna—which we can't—we'd never be allowed to with Viona and Thania on the go. As for what's next I don't know. Just have to see if anything turns up that seems exciting or interesting."

There was silence for a moment as Thania looked out onto the endless reaches of space. Then presently she turned, her face puzzled. She pointed through the window.

"What's that?" she asked in surprise.

The others looked in the direction she indicated. There was something in the infinite distances that they could not quite understand—a vast cosmic nebula, it seemed to be. But the curious thing about it was that it was shaped like a man, apparently dressed in luminous draperies and with his hands and arms extended as though supplicating for assistance.

"Some trick of the light," Abna said uncertainly. "It just can't be a man that size, and—"

He stopped. Suddenly the man had ceased to exist and in his place was a gigantic face—a hazy face, certainly, but there was no denying the details.

"Something odd going on out there in space," the Amazon said at last. "Faces and men don't appear and disappear like that without very good reason..." she glanced at Thania. "It looks as though things are not going to be so dull after all. We'd better take a closer look."

Thania gave a brief, delighted glance, and with a smile the Amazon turned to the switchboard and reset the Ultra's course.

ABOUT THE AUTHOR

British writer **JOHN RUSSELL FEARN** was born near Manchester, England, in 1908. As a child he devoured the science fiction of Wells and Verne, and was a voracious reader of the Boys' Story Papers. He was also fascinated by the cinema, and first broke into print in 1931 with a series of articles in *Film Weekly*.

He then quickly sold his first novel, *The Intelligence Gigantic*, to the American magazine, *Amazing Stories*. Over the next fifteen years, writing under several pseudonyms, Fearn became one of the most prolific contributors to all of the leading US science fiction pulps, including such legendary publications as *Astounding Stories*, *Startling Stories*, *Thrilling Wonder Stories*, and *Weird Tales*.

During the late 1940s he diversified into writing novels for the UK market, and also created his famous superwoman character, The Golden Amazon, for the prestigious Canadian magazine, the Toronto *Star Weekly*. In the early 1950s in the UK, his fifty-two novels as "Vargo Statten" were bestsellers, most notably his novelization of the film, *Creature from the Black Lagoon*.

Apart from science fiction, he had equal success with westerns, romances, and detective fiction, writing an amazing total of 180 novels—most of them in a period of just ten years—before his early death in 1960. His work has been translated into nine languages, and continues to be reprinted and read worldwide.

MORE BORGO PRESS TITLES BY JOHN RUSSELL FEARN

THE ADAM QUIRK SERIES

The Master Must Die: A Science Fiction Mystery
The Lonely Astronomer : A Science Fiction Mystery

THE ANJANI SERIES

The Gold of Akada: A Jungle Adventure Novel
Anjani the Mighty: A Lost Race Novel

THE BLACK MARIA SERIES

Black Maria, M.A.: A Classic Crime Novel
The Murdered Schoolgirl: A Classic Crime Novel
One Remained Seated: A Classic Crime Novel
Thy Arm Alone: A Classic Crime Novel
Death in Silhouette: A Classic Crime Novel

THE HERBERT THE DINOSAUR SERIES

A Thing of the Past
The Genial Dinosaur

OTHER BOOKS

1,000-Year Voyage: A Science Fiction Novel
Account Settled: A Science Fiction Mystery

Before Earth Came: Classic Science Fiction Stories
Bury the Hatchet: A Crime Tale
A Case for Brutus Lloyd: A Science Fiction Mystery
The Crimson Rambler: A Crime Novel
Don't Touch Me: A Crime Novel
Dynasty of the Small: Classic Science Fiction Stories
The Empty Coffins: A Mystery of Horror
The Fourth Door: A Mystery Novel
From Afar: A Science Fiction Mystery
Fugitive of Time: A Classic Science Fiction Novel
The G-Bomb: A Science Fiction Novel
The Haunted Gallery: Crime Stories
Here and Now: A Science Fiction Novel
Into the Unknown: A Science Fiction Tale
Last Conflict: Classic Science Fiction Stories
Legacy from Sirius: A Classic Science Fiction Novel
The Man from Hell: Classic Science Fiction Stories
The Man Who Was Not: A Crime Novel
Manton's World: A Classic Science Fiction Novel
Moon Magic: A Novel of Romance (as Elizabeth Rutland)
One Way Out: A Crime Novel (with Philip Harbottle)
Pattern of Murder: A Classic Crime Novel
Reflected Glory: A Dr. Castle Classic Crime Novel
Robbery Without Violence: Two Science Fiction Crime Stories
Rule of the Brains: Classic Science Fiction Stories
Shattering Glass: A Crime Novel
The Silvered Cage: A Scientific Murder Mystery
Slaves of Ijax: A Science Fiction Novel
Something from Mercury: Classic Science Fiction Stories
The Space Warp: A Science Fiction Novel
The Time Trap: A Science Fiction Novel
Valley of Pretenders: Classic Science Fiction Stories
Vision Sinister: A Scientific Detective Thriller
Voice of the Conqueror: A Classic Science Fiction Novel
What Happened to Hammond? A Scientific Mystery
Within That Room!: A Classic Crime Novel
World Without Chance: Classic Science Fiction Stories

www.ingramcontent.com/pod-product-compliance
Lightning Source LLC
Chambersburg PA
CBHW050756250626
47155CB00005B/2095